YA
Dix

#28

THE SIGN OF THE CROOKED ARROW

WITH only the slender clue of an arrow-shaped tie clasp, Frank and Joe Hardy pick up the trail of a cunning gang of thieves responsible for a wave of jewelry-store holdups.

But their investigations are interrupted when a desperate plea for help comes from their widowed cousin who lives on a cattle ranch in New Mexico. Frank, Joe, and their pal Chet Morton fly there immediately. The mysterious disappearance of one cowboy after another has given Crowhead Ranch the reputation of being jinxed, and it is quickly being stampeded toward financial ruin.

The young detectives face grave danger before they uncover a cleverly conceived plot engineered by the crooked arrow gang. In a dramatic climax Frank, Joe, and Chet aid law-enforcement officers in smashing the highly organized band of criminals, putting an end both to the troubles at Crowhead Ranch and the jewelry-store robberies.

An arrow whizzed past Frank's head.

Hardy Boys Mystery Stories

THE SIGN
OF THE
CROOKED ARROW

BY

FRANKLIN W. DIXON

GROSSET & DUNLAP

Publishers • New York

Printed in the United States of America

CONTENTS

THE SIGN OF THE
CROOKED ARROW

CHAPTER I

The Abandoned Car

THE Hardy boys' convertible, heading for the open country, whizzed past a road sign inscribed *Bayport City Limits*.

Dark-haired, eighteen-year-old Frank fingered the wheel lightly. Joe, who was blond and a year younger than Frank, sat beside him.

"What's all this business about somebody forgetting a car?" Joe asked.

"A man and his wife left it at Slow Mo's garage in Pleasantville two weeks ago and never called for it," Frank replied.

The boys' father, Detective Fenton Hardy, had given Frank the details of the case and suggested that his sons follow it up. The garage proprietor had appealed to Mr. Hardy to find the owner of the car.

"Why didn't Slow Mo contact the license bureau?" Joe put in.

"Dad asked him that. Slow Mo says when he went to look at the plates, they were gone!"

"Who took them off?"

"That's what we're supposed to find out," Frank said.

Half an hour later he pulled up in front of a rickety building in the sleepy town of Pleasantville.

"That must be Slow Mo," Joe observed as a gray-haired man in overalls shuffled toward them.

"Hello," he greeted them. "What can I do for you?"

When he learned who they were, he asked in surprise, "Where's your dad?"

"He's busy on another case," Joe replied. "He sent us to help you."

The old man frowned. "I sure was countin' on him. He's the best detective in this part of the country."

"You're right there," agreed Frank. "But I think Joe and I can make a start on solving the mystery. We often work with Dad on cases."

The boys' sleuthing career had begun with finding the solution to *The Tower Treasure* mystery.

Since then, their detective work had taken them all over the country and abroad as well. Recently they had uncovered *The Secret of Skull Mountain* and discovered the reason for the mysterious water shortage in town.

Slow Mo, who had been dubbed "Slow Motion" in his youth, rubbed his whiskers with a grimy finger. "Well, I dunno," he said. "But come into my office and I'll tell you what happened, anyway."

"What do the police think?" Frank inquired.

"Didn't ask them," Slow Mo replied. "Jake, the chief, is my brother-in-law. We don't get on, and I don't want to bother with him. That's why I called your dad."

The old man crossed the floor of the garage and entered a small room. It was stacked high with empty oil cans and old tires. A faded calendar, dating back three years, hung on the wall.

Joe grinned. "Don't you have one for this year?" he asked.

Slow Mo smiled sheepishly. "Never thought of that," he said and pointed to a couple of rickety chairs. "Sit down there."

The boys listened as he unfolded his story, most of which they already knew. At one point Joe interrupted to ask for a description of the couple who had left the car.

Slow Mo looked blank. "Why, they were kind of ordinary-looking folks, middle-aged, dressed like regular people—"

"Do you know where they went afterward?"

"Took a train. The station's right over there," the garageman replied. "Pleasantville's the terminal for one of the railroads," he added proudly.

"What's the engine number of the car?" Frank asked.

"I dunno," Slow Mo answered. "Guess I should've looked. Never thought of that."

At Joe's request, he led the Hardys to the rear of the garage, where a black sedan stood in a corner.

Frank threw up the hood and glanced at the engine.

"Got a flashlight?" he asked Mo.

When the proprietor handed him one, Frank scanned the motor.

"Just as I thought!" he announced. "The engine number has been filed off!"

Joe opened the door and looked for the serial number. It was missing, too.

"Why would anybody do that?" Slow Mo asked, running his fingers through his gray crew cut.

"To conceal the identity of the car," Frank explained. "This," he added, "is a case for the local police, whether you like it or not."

Slow Mo put in the call and soon afterward a short, heavy-set man puffed into the garage.

"Hello, Jake," Slow Mo said. "These are the Hardy boys. Sons of Fenton Hardy the detective."

"What have they done?" Jake asked. "Want 'em arrested?"

"No," Frank said, laughing. "We'd like you to arrest the person who filed the number off the engine of this car." He pointed to the sedan.

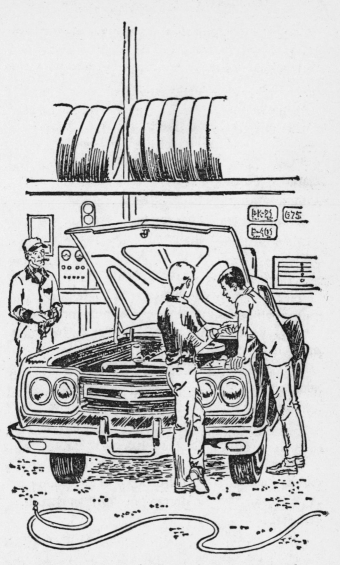

"The engine number has been filed off!" Frank
announced

"Besides, the guy that left it here owes me two weeks' rent," put in Slow Mo.

A determined look spread over the police chief's face. "I'll arrest him, all right. Where is he?"

"That's what we'd like to find out," Frank told him. "Slow Mo said he left here two weeks ago."

"Got rather a head start, didn't he?" Jake declared. He examined the car inside and out, but found nothing.

Then he took a fingerprint kit from his car and went to work on the sedan's steering wheel and dashboard.

"Most of them are smudged," he remarked. "But we'll see what we can do." He turned to Mo. "Let us know right away if somebody should claim the car, will you?" Then he said good-by and left.

Frank spoke up. "Suppose Joe and I look for some clues."

"Sure. Go ahead," the garage owner said.

Frank examined the car's upholstery, while his brother removed the mats from the floor. Then Joe opened the glove compartment. It was empty except for a narrow leather strap worn at one end. A barely discernible design had been worked into the leather.

"Looks like part of an old strap from a wrist watch," he commented, showing it to Frank. "Wonder why anyone would save it."

"It may be a valuable clue," Frank said, continuing his own search. He pulled out the back seat and ran his hand behind the upholstery. His only reward was a hairpin and a dime. Then suddenly his fingers touched a hard object. Tugging carefully, he pulled out a piece of jewelry.

"A tie clasp," Frank announced, holding up the object.

"It's an arrow, but it's crooked," Joe observed.

Slow Mo peered closely at the slightly S-shaped arrow clasp. "Probably got bent," he said.

"I don't think so," Frank replied. "Looks to me as if it had been made that way."

Pocketing the piece of strap and tie clasp, the Hardys said good-by to Slow Mo and got into their car. Just as Joe was about to start the engine, a man turned in from the road and walked into the garage.

"I wonder who that guy is," Joe asked. The stranger had broad shoulders, bushy black eyebrows, and a large nose. "Looks like a prize fighter."

The boys waited a moment. Then they heard the men's voices from inside, arguing loudly.

"We'd better see what's going on," Frank said. "Sounds as if Slow Mo's in trouble!"

They got out of their car and dashed inside. The stranger was snarling at Slow Mo.

"All right, I didn't leave it! And I don't care

if the license plates *are* gone. I'm taking that car!"

With that he gave Slow Mo a wallop. The elderly garage owner staggered backward and fell. His head struck the side of a door with a resounding crack and he sprawled unconscious.

Frank and Joe leaped forward. The burly stranger, surprised by their sudden appearance, halted abruptly. Then he whirled about and ran out the side door of the garage.

While Frank bent over Slow Mo, Joe tore after the assailant. He was only a few yards behind his quarry when the man bounded up the steps of the old Pleasantville railroad station. A train was just pulling out.

With a lunge, the man grasped the handrail on the last coach, teetered precariously a moment, then pulled himself aboard. By this time the train was moving fast.

Joe summoned all his strength for a final burst of speed and made a frantic leap!

CHAPTER II

Daylight Robbery

JOE missed the train by inches, however. Breathless and disgusted, he watched as it roared down the tracks.

Dejected, he turned and walked back to the garage. He told Frank, who was bathing Slow Mo's head with cold water, what had happened.

"How is he?" Joe asked anxiously.

"Coming to," Frank replied.

As the boys watched, Slow Mo's eyelids fluttered open.

"Wh-where am I?" he asked in a daze.

"In your office," Frank replied. "Take it easy."

"I remember now," the man said. "Big guy hit me. Where'd he go? Did he get the car?"

When Frank told him about the stranger's escape, Slow Mo sighed.

"I'm sorry he got away. But I wouldn't want anything to happen to you boys on my account."

Assured that Slow Mo was well enough to be left alone, the boys drove to police headquarters to report what had happened.

"I'll send out a seven-state alarm," the police chief said crisply. "Thanks for your help, boys."

A few minutes later Frank and Joe were headed back to Bayport.

"I don't like the looks of this, Joe," Frank said, frowning.

His brother agreed. "Do you think that guy was trying to retrieve the car for the people who left it two weeks ago?"

"Could be," Frank replied. "But why the big rush to leave the garage—unless he wanted to steal it!"

"What I'd like to know," Joe said, "is *who* took the license plates and filed off the engine number."

All the way home the boys tried vainly to figure out what was back of the mystery. "Maybe Dad'll come up with something," Joe said as they pulled into the Hardys' driveway.

They entered their father's study and found him seated in a red-leather chair poring over a dossier of criminal records.

"Hello, boys," he said. "How did you make out at Slow Mo's?"

"Dad," Frank began seriously, "there sure is something fishy about that abandoned car."

Fenton Hardy sat forward in his chair. Frank told about the stranger who had attacked Slow Mo, then showed his father the worn watch strap and the tie clasp.

His father examined the clasp, repeating the words "crooked arrow" over and over.

"What do you make of it?" Joe asked.

"Boys," replied Mr. Hardy, "I believe you've dug up a clue that may tie in with a baffling case I'm working on."

"What is it?" Frank asked eagerly.

"You've read about a series of jewelry-store robberies in and around Bayport, haven't you?"

Frank and Joe nodded as the detective went on.

"I found out that similar crime waves broke out in three other cities early this summer, and that the method is almost alike."

Joe pointed to the papers on his father's desk. "Is that what these are about?"

"Yes," Mr. Hardy replied. He reached for a folder lying on a low bookshelf behind his desk. "And here are statements from the various victims in the Bayport area."

Frank glanced over the reports. "Both here and out of state," he observed, "the victims were alone in jewelry shops when a stranger entered. They became faint and lost consciousness immediately after they had been accosted."

"Yes," said Mr. Hardy, "and as you'll see if you

read further, the victim always woke up without the slightest idea of what occurred. Then he discovered that his money and valuable jewelry were missing. And no one has been able to describe the thief sufficiently in order to give us a lead."

"Why do the people faint?" asked Joe.

"That's what I'm trying to find out, especially since there are obviously no unpleasant after-effects," his father replied. "Also, it seems that as soon as an investigation is started, the crime wave dies out, only to flare up in another city."

"Boy! These aren't conventional holdups!" Frank exclaimed, shaking his head.

"No. But they do have an oddly conventional aspect—reminds me of the old cops-and-robbers movies. In every case the victim reports that a man has approached him and asked him a question."

"A question?" Joe put in. "Not the old 'Got a match?' routine!"

"Exactly!" said Mr. Hardy. "Or the query may have to do with the time of day or the location of the nearest bus stop."

"But what makes you think this case ties in with the mystery of the car at Slow Mo's?" Frank spoke up.

Fenton Hardy smiled. "This crooked arrow tie clasp," he said. "Sam's been checking out a small restaurant on the waterfront called Mike's Place. It's a hangout for shady characters. While he was there, someone used the words 'crooked arrow' in discussing the recent jewelry-store robberies."

Sam Radley was Mr. Hardy's operative, who assisted him on his cases, and the boys knew him well.

"Crooked arrow?" Joe repeated. "Do you suppose that could be a symbol of the gang?"

Mr. Hardy shrugged. "It's possible."

Just then a tall, angular woman strode through the doorway of the study.

"Hello, Aunt Gertrude," said the boys.

"Hello," she replied, then blurted out, "Shame on you, Fenton Hardy! I just heard you talking about a new case. I suppose now you won't be going out West to visit Cousin Ruth!"

Aunt Gertrude, Mr. Hardy's unmarried sister, lived with the family and often felt it necessary to keep the male members in line, especially when Mrs. Hardy was away on a visit, which she was at present.

"Well, I—"

"It's not every day you have an invitation to visit a ranch in New Mexico!" Aunt Gertrude interrupted the detective. "And besides, you need a vacation. I'm worried about you!"

"Now, Gertrude," Mr. Hardy said soothingly, "I haven't forgotten about Ruth—it's just that I have a few important matters to tend to before I take any trip."

"Your health is important too," his sister

spluttered. With that she popped out of the room.

Frank and Joe grinned broadly. "Orders from headquarters, Dad!" Joe remarked teasingly.

"She's quite a sergeant, all right." Mr. Hardy laughed.

He opened a desk drawer and took out an aerial photo of the ranch Ruth Hardy had been running since the recent death of her husband. The boys looked over the picture and listened as the detective described the area.

Secretly Frank and Joe wished they could accompany their father to the sprawling Crowhead Ranch. Though they already had planned a camping trip with their friend Chet Morton, they gladly would have postponed it.

That evening after dinner the boys went to their crime detection lab over the garage and examined the worn watch strap. Careful scrutiny revealed no distinguishable fingerprints.

"I think we should take this strap to a chemist for analysis tomorrow," Frank suggested.

"Good idea," Joe agreed. "Maybe we can find out what kind of person wore it."

After breakfast the next morning Frank and Joe took the strap to Mr. Strand, a chemist in Bayport. He knew the boys well, and promised to have an analysis for them as soon as possible.

As they rode home through a residential area just outside of town a stoplight flashed on, and

Frank brought their car to a halt. Near the corner they noticed two men in conversation.

While the boys waited for the light to turn, one of the men walked away. A moment later the other man suddenly slumped to the sidewalk.

"Look, Joe!" Frank exclaimed. "The guy may be ill. We'd better help him."

They jumped out of the car, walked over to the man, and pulled him to his feet. As they did, he shook himself vigorously.

"Hey, leave me alone!" he ordered. "Why are you holding me?"

"You collapsed," Frank replied. "How do you feel?"

"Your friend walked away a few seconds before," Joe put in.

"He wasn't my friend," the man said irritably. "Just asked me for a light and—"

Suddenly he felt his hip pocket and looked startled. Then he grabbed Frank and Joe and bellowed:

"Help! Help! I've been robbed! Arrest these boys!"

"Let go!" Frank demanded. "We didn't take anything of yours!"

"Then where's my wallet?" the man shouted. "I just closed my store and had almost nine hundred dollars in it. I was going to take the money to the bank after lunch!"

Suddenly the answer dawned on the boys. They had witnessed one of the mysterious robberies their father had told them about!

"I'll go after the thief, Joe," Frank volunteered.

In a flash he was in the car, down the street, and out of sight, following the course taken by the suspect. Meanwhile, Joe got the full story from the victim.

"The guy asked me for a light," the man explained. "I didn't have a match, so he went on. Then I passed out."

"That's where we came in," Joe said. "We thought you were ill. Ever see the thief before?"

"No." The man, now fully recovered, said he was rough-looking and rough-mannered.

Just then Frank pulled up to the curb. He stepped out of the car, followed by a policeman.

"The thief got away," Frank reported. "I spotted him three blocks from here, because there was nobody in the street, but then he ducked into an alley and I lost him."

"I saw Frank looking for someone," the policeman put in, "and he told me what had happened."

"By the way," said Joe, addressing the stranger, "Officer Willis can vouch for us."

"Sure can." The patrolman smiled. "Every cop in town knows the Hardy boys. Great detectives!"

The policeman said that the boys would be needed as witnesses. They drove to headquarters in the Hardys' car, where Officer Willis made out a report.

Next morning after breakfast the telephone rang. Frank answered, spoke a few words, and hung up.

"It was Mr. Strand," he said to Joe. "He's completed the watch-strap analysis."

"Great!" his brother replied. "Let's go!"

Soon the boys arrived at the lab and greeted the chemist, who nodded with a smile.

"Are you boys just back from a Western trip?"

Frank and Joe exchanged puzzled glances. "No," Frank replied. "Why?"

"Indians," the chemist said. "I gather from the leather strap you brought in yesterday that you two are at work on a case involving Indians!"

CHAPTER III

Dead-End Clue

"INDIANS!" echoed Frank, completely dumb-founded. "What do you mean?"

The chemist held up the piece of leather. "This probably has been worn by an Indian."

"How can you tell?" Joe asked curiously.

Mr. Strand explained, "In the first place the tanning agents used are not the commercial variety. The leather was prepared either by an amateur, or—" He put the strap under a microscope and beckoned to Frank.

The boy adjusted his eyes to the instrument and studied the strap carefully. "I see what you mean. Definitely Indian design. Lightning, the sun, rain, and a thunderbird."

"Right," the chemist agreed. "Southwest Indian handicraft work."

"Maybe bought by a tourist," Joe suggested.

"I doubt it," the chemist went on. "Here, smell this."

The brothers looked at each other as Mr. Strand held up the strap toward their noses. Frank sniffed first. He reported a faint odor of hominy.

"Exactly," Mr. Strand said. "Indians are said to smell like that—a different body aroma."

"Mr. Strand," Frank said, "this has been interesting. Thanks a lot for your help."

"Any time," the chemist replied. "Good luck to you!"

As the two boys got into their car, Joe remarked, "The guy I chased from Slow Mo's didn't look like an Indian."

"No, but maybe an Indian owns the car."

"That silver tie clasp you found, Frank—it might have been made by an Indian."

"Say, I forgot about that," said his brother, pulling the clasp from his pocket and examining it. "Looks to me like the sort of silver work I've seen in Indian-made jewelry."

"Where to now?" Joe asked as Frank started the motor.

"Straight to Slow Mo's."

When they drew up in front of the garage, the proprietor was seated on a chair tilted against the old building.

"Solve the mystery yet?" he inquired with a grin.

"No," said Frank as he and Joe got out of the car. "We came to ask you some more questions. Did that couple who left the car look like Indians?"

"Indians?" Slow Mo pondered. "Well, the man didn't, but the woman—" He rolled his eyes. "I never thought of that. She could've been one. Had straight black hair and kinda dark skin."

"Did you hear anything more from the police?" Joe inquired.

"Jake had no luck with the fingerprints. He'll call if anything new turns up."

The boys thanked Mo and headed back to Bayport. If the garage owner's memory served him correctly, they had a good clue.

"We'll have to be on the lookout for Indians," Frank mused on the way.

Suddenly Joe exclaimed, "I just had a brain storm! Why don't we look for the watch that went with the band we found? It may still have the other piece of the strap attached to it!"

"Okay by me," his brother agreed. "But how about some lunch first?"

After a brief stop for hamburgers, the boys began their search. First they went to all the jewelry repair shops in town, where Frank posed the same question:

"Do you have a watch with a broken strap to fit this piece?" The answer was invariably a "no."

Next, they looked at scores of watches at second-hand shops, but with no results.

"Only one thing left." Joe sighed. "Pawn-shops!"

"Right. Let's try the one down there."

The boys gazed into the window of Maxby's dingy store, then entered. Frank tossed the routine question.

"Think I have."

"May we see it?" Joe asked eagerly.

The pawnbroker went to the back of the store and came out with a man's wrist watch. Part of the leather strap that flopped from it matched the piece Frank held!

"We've found it!" Joe exulted.

Frank said nothing. As the shopkeeper looked on curiously, he examined the watch and uttered a sharp exclamation.

"What's the matter?" Joe asked.

"Look!" Frank cried, pointing.

Across the top, etched into the design around the face of the watch, was a crooked arrow!

In amazement Frank and Joe studied the sweeping S.

"Find an heirloom?" asked the pawnbroker.

"No," answered Frank, "just an old watch we've been hunting for. Where did you get this?"

"I'll check," the man answered, thumbing through a worn ledger. "Let's see—"

The shopkeeper went back day after day until he stopped at a page bearing the same date as the day the black sedan had been left in Slow Mo's garage—seventeen days previously!

"Here it is," he said. "This watch was pawned by Annie Groves, 66 Fern Terrace."

"Did she look like an Indian?" Joe queried.

"She didn't look Indian to me," replied the man.

"By the way," he added, "this isn't—er—a stolen watch, is it?"

Frank told the man he had no idea. Then, after thanking him for his trouble, he and Joe hastily left the store.

"Let's get to 66 Fern Terrace quick!" Frank said. "I'd like to meet this Annie Groves."

Joe took the wheel and headed for the outskirts of Bayport. Soon he turned into a street bearing the sign *Fern Terrace*.

Frank spotted the even numbers on the left side of the road. "Here's 50," he said. "And 62," he added as the car inched along. Suddenly he exclaimed, "Joe, there isn't any 66!"

The lot where number 66 would be was vacant. A tangle of weeds covered the ground.

"A phony address," Frank said in disgust.

Joe turned the car around and went back to the business section. "Let's go to the pawnshop again and ask Maxby some more questions!"

"Not now," Frank said as they pulled up. "It's

six o'clock. He's closed. Besides, Aunt Gertrude will have dinner ready, and we'd better not keep her waiting! We can come back tomorrow."

Frank and Joe could hardly wait to finish their breakfast the next morning, so eager were they to rush off to Maxby's. Half an hour later they drove up to the pawnshop. The proprietor was surprised to see them again.

"Want to look at another watch?" he asked.

"No," Frank replied. "We want to find out who Annie Groves is."

"I gave you her address," the man said.

"It's a fake," Joe told him. "There isn't any house number 66!"

"No fault of mine," the man countered.

"We know that," Frank replied politely. "But we've got to find this woman. Perhaps you can help by giving us a description."

"What's wrong? She owe you money?"

"No." Frank laughed.

The man hesitated a moment. "Well, this Annie is a character."

"You mean she's rather peculiar?" Joe asked.

"Yeah, kinda. She's always coming around with stuff to pawn."

Suddenly the shopkeeper grabbed Frank's arm. "Say, look!" he shouted. "There she goes now!"

Frank and Joe wheeled around and caught a fleeting glimpse of a woman passing the shop-window. When the boys rushed out, she was only a few paces down the street. They caught up to her, and Frank, a trifle embarrassed, spoke up.

"Beg your pardon, Miss Groves. There's something we'd like to ask you."

The startled woman looked at them with wild eyes. Her face was neither young nor old. She wore a tattered dress, and her graying hair was untidy, hanging in wisps over her face.

"What d'you want?" she asked abruptly.

"We'd like to know where you got the wrist watch you pawned a couple of weeks ago at Maxby's," Frank said.

"What's it to you?"

"Then you did pawn a watch?" Joe queried.

"No."

"The records show you did," Frank said quietly. "You'd better tell us the truth."

"I won't tell nobody nuthin'," the woman said defiantly. "Now go away and don't bother me."

As Annie Groves started to push past the boys, Frank said:

"Well, the police might like to ask you a few questions if you don't tell us."

The word "police" worked like magic. "Oh, no, please." Then Annie Groves added nervously, "I'll tell you where I got the watch—I found it."

"Where?" Joe asked.

"Right in front of Jenk's Tobacco Shop."

With that Annie turned on her heels and hurried down the street.

"What do you make of it?" Joe asked.

"She might be mixed up with some of that crooked arrow mob," Frank ventured, "judging from the way she jumped at the mention of the police."

"Strike one," said Joe. "And why did she give Maxby a fake address? Let's take a run over to police headquarters and check on her."

Shortly afterward, the boys walked into the office of their friend Police Chief Collig. The husky man greeted them cordially.

"What can I do for you?" he asked with a broad grin.

"We'd like to find out something about an Annie Groves," Frank replied.

"That's easy enough," the chief replied. "Nothing particularly wrong with Annie—just a harmless vagrant."

"Is she mixed up with any gang?" Joe queried.

"No," the chief said, "not that we know of. She spends most of her time pawning things she finds on the street."

"Well, that seems to clear Annie," Joe said as the boys left headquarters.

"But she did add a couple of clues to the case," Frank remarked.

"That's right," Joe agreed. "Since she pawned the watch on the same day the mystery car was left in Slow Mo's garage, the owner must have had business in Bayport."

"Maybe in Jenk's Tobacco Shop," Frank said, recalling where Annie had found the watch.

"Jenk might be mixed up with the gang," Joe ventured. "I recall he once had a partner who served time in prison. When that fellow was around, the tobacco store was a meeting place for all kinds of shady characters."

"Jenk might even own a watch with a crooked arrow on it!" Frank added. "Let's go!"

The boys went to the tawdry little store, located in the waterfront district of Bayport. A few rough-looking characters stood outside.

"Here's where we get tough," Joe said, grinning.

As they strode into the dimly lighted store, Joe addressed the bald, heavy-set man behind the counter. "You Jenk?"

"Yeah!"

"I'd like a pack of cigarettes."

Jenk looked at the boys with narrowed eyes. "I don't sell to minors," he said firmly.

"Have it your way." Joe shrugged. "We'll go somewhere else."

"Say, you got the time?" Frank asked suddenly, leaning over the counter toward the man.

Jenk obligingly held out his hand. But the watch revealed no crooked arrow.

"If you can tell time," Jenk said sarcastically, "you can see it's ten o'clock. Time for fresh kids to scram. Now get goin'!"

Frank and Joe returned to their car and drove home.

Disappointed that nothing had come of their clue, the boys were anxious to discuss the case with their father. Soon Frank parked the car in the garage and they entered the hallway.

"I hope Dad's here," Joe said, walking instinctively toward the telephone table to check for messages. "Hey, what's this!" he exclaimed. "Mother's writing!"

"She must be back from her trip," Frank remarked. "What does it say, Joe?"

The boys gazed at the memo pad, then gasped. Written in a hurried hand was a note that stunned them:

Your father in Bayport General Hospital. Shot. Come at once!

CHAPTER IV

Distressing News

"Dad in the hospital!" Joe cried in disbelief.

The boys stared at the terse note. There was no mistaking the news.

"This is Mom's handwriting, all right," Frank declared. "Aunt Gertrude's not here, either. Come on, Joe. Let's get over there!"

Ten minutes later they entered the hospital and spoke to the receptionist.

"We're Fenton Hardy's sons," Frank said. "We'd like to see him right away."

The woman looked in her files, then said, "You may visit him for a few minutes. Room 328."

Their footsteps echoed hollowly as they approached the door of the room. A screen concealed the patient, and the boys heard low voices behind it. Together they stepped around the partition and stood beside the bed.

On it lay their father, pale and restless. His

eyes were closed and he was breathing heavily. Standing beside him were his wife, Aunt Gertrude, a young doctor, and a nurse.

"What happened?" Frank asked in a hoarse whisper.

"Mr. Hardy hasn't wakened from the anesthetic yet," the doctor said. "Bad wound in his leg. He's lost a lot of blood."

"Wound?" Joe repeated in a shaky voice. "Is it—serious?"

"Yes," the doctor replied quietly. "But your father should be all right soon, provided no complications set in."

Mrs. Hardy took each of her sons by the arm and guided them into the hall.

"Tell us about it," Frank pleaded.

"How many bullets hit Dad?" Joe put in.

"Oh, he wan't shot by a gun," their mother replied. "He was—"

"Mrs. Hardy." It was the doctor's voice. "Your husband wants to see you all." They hurried back into the room.

Fenton Hardy had heard the voices of his boys and had roused sufficiently to call them. Now he was completely awake, and had opened his eyes.

"Dad!" Frank whispered, leaning forward.

Joe pressed close to Frank. "How are you, Dad?"

"I'm all right," Mr. Hardy said, forcing a smile. "I'll be up and out of here in no time."

"Mother says you weren't shot by a gun," Frank said. "What *did* hit you?"

"An arrow."

The boys' mouths dropped open in amazement.

"It hit him high in the left leg," the doctor said. "A nasty wound, deep to the bone."

Aunt Gertrude continued the story. "Your father said he was investigating a vacant house on the outskirts of town. He thought some of the thieves were using it as a hideout."

"Were they inside?" Joe asked.

"No," continued their aunt. "The place was empty, but just after your father left the house, he was struck from behind by an arrow."

Mr. Hardy carried on. "Then I staggered to the road for help."

"Did you see who shot you?" Joe asked.

"No, son," he replied. "He must have been hiding in the bushes behind the house."

The physician interrupted. "That's all for now, please. Mr. Hardy must rest."

"You boys go along with Aunt Gertrude," Mrs. Hardy said. "I'm going to stay here."

The three left quietly. At the hospital entrance they met Sam Radley.

"How is he?" Sam asked worriedly. "I just heard about the accident."

Frank told the tall, sandy-haired investigator all he knew. Sam's brow furrowed.

"Incredible!" he remarked with deep concern.

"Why would anybody shoot him with an arrow?" Joe wondered aloud.

"Probably," Sam replied, "to escape detection. An arrow will be harder to trace than a bullet. Where is the arrow?"

"At police headquarters," Aunt Gertrude said. "Fenton had it sent there immediately."

"We'd better take a look at it," Sam said.

He took Aunt Gertrude in his car, and the boys drove to headquarters in their convertible. On the way, Frank said to Joe, "You thinking the same thing I am?"

"I'll say!" Joe replied. "The arrow!"

"That's it," Frank said. "First Sam picks up the words 'crooked arrow' at Mike's Place, then we find the crooked arrow on the watch and tie clasp. And now Dad is shot with an arrow!"

"It all adds up to a big question mark," Joe declared. "Only one thing's clear. Someone wants Dad out of his way."

The two cars arrived at headquarters about the same time. Aunt Gertrude, Sam, and the boys were ushered into the office of Chief Collig, who sat at his desk examining the arrow.

"Hello there," he said. "Awfully sorry to hear about your father, boys."

"Thanks," Frank replied. "Any clues yet?"

"None at all. My men searched the deserted house and found a trampled spot in the weeds where the culprit may have hidden, but nothing else."

"May I see the arrow, Chief?" Frank asked.

Collig handed him a short thick shaft with a sharp steel tip. On the end, near the nock, were three white feathers.

"This could kill a man!" Frank exclaimed.

"Sure could," Collig agreed. "Your father was mighty lucky."

"Look at those feathers," Joe observed. "They're all the same color."

"Aren't they supposed to be?" Aunt Gertrude asked.

"Two are usually the same color, such as red," Joe explained. "The other, known as the cock feather, stands at right angles to the nock, and is of a different color."

"Then an expert archer must have shot this arrow," Frank concluded. "He didn't need a colored feather to show him which was the cock feather."

"Right," Sam said. "And he didn't mean to kill your father, just incapacitate him. Well, we've got to look for an expert archer."

"We could start on the Indians in town," Frank suggested, giving Joe a significant glance.

"There are only four in Bayport," the chief told the boys. "We've checked them out already, and they seem to be upstanding citizens. But bear in mind that Indians aren't the only ones expert with a bow."

"You're right. It's like looking for a needle in a haystack," Frank mused.

"Do you mind if we look up the Indians, anyway, Chief?" Joe asked. "Perhaps one of them had a relative visiting, who would bear investigating."

"By all means, go ahead," Collig replied and gave him a list of names.

After bidding the chief and Sam good-by, Frank and Joe took Aunt Gertrude home for lunch. Then they started out to question the four local Indians. All were skilled at trades and had good jobs. None had visitors and none had ever handled a bow in his life.

"Looks as if we've reached a dead end," Frank said disappointedly.

"What next?" Joe asked.

"I don't know yet. But we'd better forget about that camping trip with Chet. Let's drive out to his place and tell him."

Joe nodded, and soon Frank pulled up alongside the porch of the Morton farmhouse, which was located several miles out of town. Iola, Chet's pretty sister and Joe's favorite date, greeted them with a smile.

"Hi!" shouted Joe. "Where's Chet?"

"Behind the barn," she replied.

Frank parked, and the boys made their way to the back. They spied their stocky, good-natured friend crouching like a football lineman. Rushing at him was a big man, his muscular arms outstretched.

Then, faster than the eye could follow, he grabbed Chet and flipped him up into the air! The boy landed on the ground with a thud. Frank and Joe rushed to his aid.

"Oh, hi there," Chet said casually and picked himself up. Then he introduced the young man who had thrown him. "This is Russ Griggs. He's teaching me judo!"

"We thought he was attacking you!" Joe said.

Russ laughed. "Chet's a pretty good pupil, but quite a load! We were just working on a movement against the back."

"We know a couple of judo holds," Frank said, "but that last one you used on Chet was a beauty!"

"It's easy enough, if you're fast," Russ replied. "Here, I'll show you how it goes."

Frank stepped forward and the man showed him the fundamentals of the hold, taking each step slowly.

"Now try it on me," he said.

Hardly were the words out of his mouth when the husky Russ went zooming through the air like a rocket.

"Hey!" he shouted to Frank. "*I'm* the instructor, remember?"

They laughed, and the judo expert showed them a variety of other holds. Then he said good-by.

After Russ had left, the boys gathered on the spacious porch. Frank and Joe quickly told Chet about their baffling case and of the attack on their father.

"Shot by an arrow!" Chet exclaimed, and added, "Gosh, I'm sure sorry, fellows."

"We'll have to postpone our camping trip," Joe announced.

"Oh, sure, I understand."

Presently the telephone rang, and Mrs. Morton called, "It's for you, Frank."

He went inside, spoke a few words, and came back to the porch.

"It was Slow Mo," he said to Joe. "He's dug up some new info and wants to see us."

"How'd he know you were here?" Chet asked.

"Aunt Gertrude told him," Frank explained. "We'd better go."

Frank and Joe drove off to Pleasantville. As they stopped in front of the garage, Slow Mo ambled out to meet them.

"More funny business goin' on around here," he announced.

"What happened?"

"Some smart aleck tried to take that car last night," he replied. "But I fooled him."

"How?" Joe asked.

Slow Mo scratched his whiskers and grinned. "Well, he got in a window, but when he tried to open the garage doors my burglar alarm went off and scared him away!"

"Good for you!" Frank said. "I didn't know you had an alarm."

"Oh, I didn't till a few days ago," Slow Mo replied. He looked a little sheepish. "Never thought of it until all this trouble started over the black sedan."

The boys exchanged grins, then the three went into the garage and looked around. The mystery car was halfway across the floor. The intruder evidently had moved it before trying to open the garage doors.

"Did you find any clues?" Frank queried.

"Nothin'," Slow Mo said, " 'cept the fellow must be a chicken farmer."

"What makes you think that?" Joe asked.

"He left a feather on the seat of the car," Slow Mo replied. He reached an oily hand into his pocket and drew out a smudged white feather.

"Boy!" Joe exclaimed. "What a clue!"

"A clue?" Slow Mo looked puzzled. "Never thought of that."

Frank and Joe thanked Slow Mo for the information and headed back to Bayport.

"I think we have something here," Frank remarked. "This feather sure looks like the ones on the arrow that wounded Dad."

After parking in front of police headquarters, the boys hurried inside. The chief was not there, but the sergeant in charge let them examine the arrow again. Frank compared the feathers.

"Look, Joe!" he said excitedly. "They match!"

"Then the guy who dropped this at Slow Mo's may be the one who shot Dad!" Joe exclaimed. "We've got to find him!"

At the mention of Mr. Hardy, the sergeant pricked up his ears. "Too bad about that latest news," he declared. "I know how you must feel."

"Too bad about what?" Frank asked quickly.

"Haven't you heard?" the officer asked in surprise. "The arrow that shot your father was poisoned!"

CHAPTER V

Expensive Evidence

WITHOUT waiting for another word, Frank and Joe ran to their car and drove to the hospital in record time. When they reached their father's room, they found him very ill. Mrs. Hardy was by his side.

"Your father was poisoned by that arrow," she said a bit shakily. "The doctors are doing all they can."

Mr. Hardy was too weak to speak, but he smiled faintly at his sons.

"You'd better go along," Mrs. Hardy said presently. "I'll phone the house if I need you."

Deeply worried, the boys drove home and telephoned the details of their visit to Sam Radley. Later, Mrs. Hardy called from the hospital that their father was somewhat improved, but that she would stay with him. The boys ate dinner with Aunt Gertrude and went directly to bed.

The following morning their mother had an encouraging report on Mr. Hardy. This buoyed their spirits considerably.

"Joe," said Frank, getting up from the breakfast table, "we'll have to think of a new approach on how to locate those holdup men."

"You're right," Joe agreed. "Tell you what. Let's go down to Mike's Place and ask people in that area for the time. Maybe—just maybe—we'll find another wrist watch with a crooked arrow or a lead to the thieves who use that question as a gimmick."

The Hardys drove to the street where the restaurant was located and parked their car. Then they began the tedious job of questioning the passers-by. As the hours wore on, the answer was usually a polite "twelve-thirty," "one-fifteen," "three forty-five." Still the boys persisted.

About four o'clock, Frank, across the street from where Joe was standing, stopped a short, husky fellow who wore a cap pulled low on his forehead. Instead of giving him the time, the man growled, "Get out of my way!"

Frank stepped toward the man, who suddenly cocked his arm. A heavy fist flashed. Before the boy could duck, the blow caught him on the point of the chin. Stunned, he staggered backward against a building!

"Stop him!" Joe shouted as the man dashed down the street.

But the few people who had witnessed the scene merely stared, letting the stranger escape.

"I'll get him!" Joe cried, racing to his brother's side. "Meet you at the car," he told Frank, who by this time had regained his balance.

The squat man was a block ahead when Joe spotted him snaking among the pedestrians.

The boy gained yard after yard, leaving a trail of gaping onlookers. Presently he found himself only a block away from Jenk's Tobacco Shop!

Hearing Joe's footsteps close behind, Frank's attacker put on an extra burst of speed. A moment later he dashed into the tobacco store. When Joe ran through the doorway, his quarry was leaning against the counter, puffing madly.

"What's the idea of hitting my brother?" the boy demanded, clenching his fists.

"Your—your brother's too nosy," the short man wheezed. "Tried to look at my watch—and I don't even have one on."

Joe glanced at the man's wrists. There was no watch. But he noted a section of slightly untanned skin on his left arm as if one had been worn recently.

"You *had* a watch on," Joe retorted. "What did you do with it?"

Jenk, who was standing behind the counter, looked at Joe. "That fresh kid again," he said menacingly. "You got an unhealthy interest in the time. Why don't you chase along home?"

Stunned, Frank staggered backward

Joe had all he could do to keep from taking a punch at both men. But he knew he would be no match for Jenk and the stranger.

"Okay," he said, and walked out.

But he had no intention of dropping the matter. The fact that the chase had led to the tobacco shop was too good a clue to abandon.

Joe hurried to the place where the boys had parked their car. Frank was waiting.

"Find out anything, Joe?" he asked. "I thought maybe something had happened to you."

His brother quickly brought him up to date.

"We've got to investigate Jenk's place thoroughly," he said. "I have a feeling he's connected in some way with the Bayport holdup gang."

"It's a sure bet Jenk won't give *us* any information," Frank reasoned. "He's seen too much of us already."

"I've got it!" Joe exclaimed. "We'll send Chet!"

"Good idea," Frank agreed with a laugh. "Jenk wouldn't suspect him. He looks too innocent."

In a few minutes the telephone rang at the Morton farm. Chet answered.

"Hi, Frank," he said cheerfully. "What's new on the case?"

"That's why I called," Frank began. "We've got a little job for you."

"Oh, oh!" said Chet. "I knew this was coming!"

Frank quickly outlined what he wanted his chum to do. Chet did not sound enthusiastic.

"What's the matter?" Frank asked. "Scared?"

"Those are pretty tough guys in that end of town," Chet protested.

"You can handle them," Frank replied. "What about those judo lessons?"

"Oh, yeah, I forgot." Chet laughed nervously.

"Okay," Frank said, "then it's a deal. See you tomorrow morning at ten at our house. Joe and I want to stop at the hospital first."

Chet arrived at the Hardys' a little early and managed to pack away a second breakfast.

"You're supposed to be reducing," Frank reminded him.

Chet grimaced. "You'd better humor me if you want me to do your dirty work for you," he declared. "Say, how's your dad?"

"Much better, thanks," Frank replied. "He sure gave us a scare, though."

As the three boys started off a few minutes later, Frank outlined their plan.

"Joe will keep an eye on the front door," he said, "I'll station myself in the delivery alley at the back."

"And I?" Chet asked apprehensively.

"You go inside," Frank continued, "and see if you can spot anything to do with a crooked arrow. Also, try to find out if Jenk's selling anything besides tobacco."

"M—maybe you'd better go in," Chet said a bit shakily, "and I'll stand guard."

"Why, Chet," Joe said with a straight face, "you're not going to back out, are you?"

"All right, all right," Chet gave in.

Frank parked the car a block from the scene. Joe stood in a doorway almost directly across the street from the shop and Frank concealed himself behind three tall ashcans in back of the building. Chet, summoning his courage, entered the store. All had agreed to meet ten minutes later in a diner down the street.

But they did not have to wait that long. Frank heard the back screen door of Jenk's shop bang shut. Poking his head around one of the cans to get a better view, he saw the same short, muscular-looking man who had socked him the previous day! The fellow stopped momentarily, glanced quickly around, then quietly slipped down the alley.

Hardly had the man disappeared when the sound of angry words and scuffling issued from the shop. Frank could hear Jenk growl in a low tone and Chet reply in a high-pitched voice.

"Let go of me!" Chet cried. "If you don't I'll— I'll—"

A crash followed and the screen door flew open. A blurred figure bounced into the alley, rolling nearly to the ashcans.

"Chet!" Frank whispered, standing up from his hiding place. "What happened?"

"Tell you later," Chet puffed. "Let's get out of here!"

Frank led the way, with Chet limping behind. They soon came to the diner where Joe was waiting. He told of having seen the man enter the store just before Chet did.

"That's right," said Chet. "Jenk was waiting on him when I stepped in. Called him Bearcat. They didn't notice me."

"Did you hear anything?" Frank asked quickly.

"Bearcat said 'Got any arrows?'" Chet related. "Jenk handed him a small package, but I didn't get a good look at it."

"Arrows!" Joe gasped. "Go on. What happened next?"

"Bearcat said, 'I'll be at Mike's,' and went out the back door," Chet replied. "Then Jenk saw me. When I said I wanted some cigars for my dad, he got mad. Threw me out before I had a chance to protest. Said kids were a pest and I was too young to be buying cigars, and—well, I guess I interrupted something that made him sore."

"It's something to do with arrows, that's for sure," Frank declared.

"Whatever these arrows are, they're small," Chet said. "And where is Mike's?"

"Just a couple of blocks from here," Frank replied. "It's a cheap restaurant by the waterfront—

the place where Sam picked up the words 'crooked arrow.' "

"Let's go!" Joe urged.

"No," Frank warned. "You and I were hanging around there yesterday and might arouse suspicion. Chet, are you game? If you're not back in fifteen minutes, we'll come after you."

"Now listen, guys. I've no great desire to be kicked out again—"

"Come on, Chet. This may be our only chance," Joe pleaded. "We'll wait for you here."

Chet grumbled, but did not let his friends down. Slowly he walked down the street, apprehensive about the man called Bearcat.

Soon he stood in front of Mike's Place. Several tough-looking men walked in and out.

"Guess I'd better act the part," Chet thought, summoning his courage. He quickly unbuttoned his collar and thrust his hands into his pockets. Then he walked boldly into the restaurant.

At first he could barely see anything in the place, which was dimly lighted and filled with cigarette smoke. As his eyes became accustomed to the gloom, he scanned the faces of the men sitting at the various tables. None resembled the short, muscular suspect he sought.

Disappointed, Chet worked his way toward the back of the restaurant. Then he spotted a booth at the extreme rear. In it sat Bearcat!

The boy slipped into the seat opposite him. Bearcat hardly noticed him as he read the menu. When he finally glanced up, Chet leaned forward.

"Say, Jenk ain't got no more arrows," Chet whispered. "How about lettin' me have one?"

The man's eyes narrowed suspiciously. Then he reached into his pocket and drew out a cigarette. Chet opened his wallet and laid a five-dollar bill on the table. To his amazement the man gave him no change.

"Jenk sure is a gyp," whined Chet. "A guy can't get far with one arrow."

"Ain't his fault," Bearcat replied.

"Thanks," Chet said, pocketing the cigarette and rising to leave.

Then he stopped short. Coming in the front door was Jenk himself. As he headed for Bearcat's booth, the boy slipped out of it, concealing himself behind a hefty waiter. Fortunately, it took a few seconds for Jenk's eyes to adjust to the dimness and he did not notice Chet heading for the door.

"Hey you," the gruff voice of the cashier called. "Pay up!"

"I didn't order anything," Chet objected shakily.

"Oh no? Say, kid, you pay or—"

Jenk had stopped to listen to the argument. Chet was fearful. He threw a bill to the cashier and hurried out to the street, running toward the diner where Frank and Joe were waiting. In his hand he held a most important clue!

At last he knew what the mysterious gimmick was—a cigarette!

As Chet neared the diner he turned the cigarette over in his fingers to inspect it.

Suddenly he saw black spots before his eyes. His head swam, then he slumped to the sidewalk!

CHAPTER VI

Police Raid

"CHET, Chet! What's the matter?" Joe bent over his friend, his face tense and worried.

"I . . . I . . . wh . . . where am I?" Chet asked, regaining consciousness.

"You're on the sidewalk," Joe replied. "When you didn't show up, Frank and I started looking for you."

With Joe's aid, Chet struggled to his feet. As his brain cleared, he told briefly what had happened at Mike's Place.

"I was on my way back to meet you fellows," he said. "I took a look at the cigarette I was holding, and then— Hey, where is it?"

"This it?" Joe asked, picking up a cigarette that had rolled into the gutter.

"Yes," Chet replied.

"Let's examine that thing carefully—but not

here," Frank said. "We'd better take it to the police.

The three drove quickly to headquarters. On the way Chet related in detail his experience in the restaurant and how he had paid five dollars for the Arrow cigarette.

"I'm sure this cigarette put you to sleep," Frank declared. "And if it did, we may have the key to the Bayport robberies."

The boys were excited as they entered the building. "This is top secret," Frank said as Chief Collig greeted the trio. The officer motioned for the doors to be closed.

Then he turned to the boys. "Have you or Sam located the man who shot your father?" he asked with quickening interest.

"No," Frank replied. "But we've uncovered a clue that may solve the mysterious robberies around Bayport."

He pulled the cigarette from his pocket and laid it on the chief's desk.

"What's this—a joke?" Collig asked.

"It's no joke," Frank insisted. "This is a cigarette that can put you to sleep!"

"What?"

"That's what happened to Chet." Frank hastily related the story of the scene in Jenk's Tobacco Shop, and concluded with Chet's adventure in the restaurant.

"I'll have this Arrow analyzed at once," declared Chief Collig. "Don't touch it. I'll get the head of our crime lab." He pressed a button on his intercom.

"Send Creech in to see me," Collig ordered.

A few minutes later a baldheaded man wearing tortoise-shell glasses entered the office.

"I'd like you to analyze this cigarette for me," the officer said.

"Okay, Chief," Creech answered. "I'll do it right away."

Shortly he returned holding a white sheet of cardboard in his hand. On it were the component parts of the cigarette.

"Here we are," he said. "This sure is a humdinger! There's genuine tobacco at both ends," he explained, pointing to the shreds of tobacco leaf on the white cardboard. "But in the middle there's a clever gadget."

"What is it?" Joe asked quickly.

Creech held a little plastic capsule between his fingers. It was about an inch long. At one end was a tiny stem.

"What on earth is all this?" Collig wondered.

"A type of bomb," the technician said. "It could hold a liquid or a gas. And the stem is a plunger. One end of it is flush with one end of the cigarette."

"Would it release whatever's inside the capsule?" Joe asked.

"Right," Creech replied. "Pressure on the

plunger trips a spring inside the tiny vial to free the gas or liquid."

"Boys, you've really come up with a lulu," Collig said. Then he thanked Creech and dismissed him.

"This cigarette," Joe began, "is being used by criminals to knock out their victims."

"And when I pressed the plunger by accident, I saw spots before my eyes and keeled over," Chet put in.

"This must be kept secret," Collig said. "Aside from your father and Sam Radley, no one should be told about it."

As the three agreed, Chet added, "Wonder what kind of anesthetic the thieves use. It had no lasting effect on me. I feel fine now."

"Some kind of ether-like gas, no doubt. Creech can check that out for us by analyzing the capsule," the chief remarked.

Again Collig pressed a button on his desk. "Jenk's store must be raided at once," he told the boys as the door opened and a sergeant entered. "Want to come along?"

"You bet! But we'll have to hurry. Bearcat probably mentioned Chet to Jenk, so he's tipped off by now," Frank said.

The police and the three boys sped to the tobacco shop.

Chief Collig's aide deftly steered their big black sedan through the downtown traffic and headed for the waterfront. Within minutes they pulled up in front of Jenk's. In a moment other carloads of police joined them.

"Nobody's here!" exclaimed Collig, opening the door.

"Hey, smells like something's burning!" Frank cried out.

He ran to the back door and looked into the alley, just in time to see Jenk hotfooting it away. A smoldering package lay on the ground.

"Stop!" Frank shouted at him.

As he called, two policemen appeared at the end of the alley, cutting off the man's escape. They collared Jenk at once and brought him to Chief Collig.

Frank stamped out the fire in the package, most of which had been reduced to char.

"Look here, Chief!" he exclaimed, kicking what was left to one side and holding a cigarette at arm's length. "They're Arrows!"

"What does this mean?" Chief Collig growled, addressing the surly Jenk.

"I ain't done nuthin'," the man protested. "Just burned some stale cigarettes."

Joe took one of them in his fingers. It had been burned halfway through. Inside was a capsule, which smoldered with a peculiar odor.

"Of course," he cried out. "This plastic burns! Jenk was trying to destroy evidence."

Collig ordered that handcuffs be put on Jenk.

"Come on!" he said. "You've got a. lot of explaining to do at headquarters!"

"I ain't got nuthin' to explain," the man declared sullenly.

Meanwhile, other police officers had searched the store. They had found nothing but a meager stock of popular brands of tobacco and cigarettes. Jenk had burned all the telltale evidence!

"We'll take this man with us," Chief Collig told the sergeant.

The Hardys said good-by to the officers and took Chet to their house, where he had left his car that morning. They had a quick lunch, then drove to the hospital.

Mr. Hardy, who was improving slowly, listened with great interest to their account of the discovery of the Arrow cigarettes.

"There's one thing we must do soon," he said.

"I think I know what you mean," Frank said. "Rout out all the Arrow cigarettes in this area, and see if we can pick up any clues to where they come from."

"Right. Get in touch with Sam. He might be able to give you a hand."

Next morning, Frank and Joe called Sam Radley, and the three set out to search for more Arrow cigarettes.

While the local police undertook to do the job in Bayport, Sam and the boys drove to the nearby towns which also had experienced an outbreak of holdups.

They stopped in all sorts of shops where cigarettes might be sold, asking the same question.

"Have you any Arrows? Jenk sent us."

Time after time the boys, working apart from Sam, were met by vacant stares and "Don't know what you're talking about!"

But in Green Point, near Pleasantville, a tobacco shopman replied, "Jenk sent you?"

"Yep," Frank answered, his pulse quickening.

"Got anything to show?"

"Crooked arrow!" Joe said, hoping that might be a password.

"Good enough for me," was the reply.

With that the man gave the boys two cigarettes, for which they paid ten dollars. The shopkeeper leaned close to the boys.

"Tell Jenk those are my last two," he whispered. "Have him send Arrow Charlie around with a new lot next time he or his pals come East."

Frank and Joe looked as casual as they could, though their pulses were racing.

"Arrow Charlie?" said Frank. "Oh, sure. Say, did he get that name from selling Arrows, or is he handy with a bow?"

The man smirked. "You ought to know!" he said conclusively.

That was enough for the Hardys. They hurried

to their car, where Sam was already waiting. He had had no luck. Frank showed him the two Arrows triumphantly, then they sped back toward the city to report the Green Point tobacconist and turn over the cigarettes for analysis.

As they rode down the road that ran past the Morton farm, they saw Chet on the porch. When they tooted their horn, the stout boy waved frantically. Frank jammed on the brakes and Chet puffed up to them, a worried look on his face.

"Your mother phoned here a few minutes ago trying to get hold of you!" he panted.

"What's wrong?" Joe asked.

"Is Dad worse?" Frank gasped.

"I don't know," Chet replied. "All she said was to come to the hospital and hurry!"

CHAPTER VII

Another Puzzle

"Thanks," Frank said. "We'll drive right over. I'll call you if anything is wrong."

He was off in a flash. The car's speedometer hovered at the legal limit as Frank and Joe raced to Bayport Hospital.

To their surprise, they found their father sitting up in his room. He greeted them cheerfully.

"Hello, boys," he called out. "Hope I didn't alarm you by asking you to come quickly."

"To be honest, you did," Frank panted. "It certainly is good to see you so chipper, though."

Joe went to the far side of his father's bed. "Gosh, you look like yourself again. Doesn't he, Mother?"

Mrs. Hardy smiled in agreement. She was pouring water for one of the many bouquets her husband had received.

"The reason I called you," Mr. Hardy said, "is

this." He held up an air-mail letter. "It's from Cousin Ruth. Some mysterious happenings at the ranch have her worried. Seems some of her best cowhands have disappeared, one by one, without a trace."

"Has she notified the local authorities?" Joe asked.

"Yes. But she has had no luck so far," his father replied. "She wants me to come immediately. Since I can't, I'd like you to fly out in my place. Take Chet, too, if he wants to go."

"We'll leave as soon as possible," Frank assured him. "There's only one thing—Joe and I just got a hot lead on the crooked arrow mystery. We'd sure like to follow it up."

"I'll put Sam Radley on your new lead," Mr. Hardy said. "Besides, I hope to be out of here soon, so I can work with him. Now tell me what you've learned."

Frank reported their experience with the Green Point tobacco dealer and his mention of Arrow Charlie.

"It sounds to us as if he's the main distributor," Frank said. "And obviously he comes East once in a while."

Mr. Hardy looked thoughtful. "I wonder where he is now."

"Have the police been able to get any information from Jenk?" Frank asked.

Mr. Hardy shook his head. "The prisoner isn't talking."

"Come on, Frank," Joe put in. "We'd better go see about those plane reservations for the trip to Cousin Ruth's."

Before leaving the hospital, Frank telephoned Chet about the proposed Western trip. Their pal eagerly accepted the invitation.

The boys had a hasty lunch at a coffee shop, and then drove to the Bayport Air Terminal. Striding up to the ticket office, Frank and Joe approached one of the clerks.

"We'd like three reservations to Albuquerque as soon as we can get them," Frank said.

The clerk examined his schedule. "Sorry," he said. "Everything's booked for a week."

"A week!" groaned Joe. "How about a plane to another point and a transfer?"

The clerk shook his head. "The schedule West is full."

"All right," Frank sighed. "Put us on the list for cancellations." He gave the man their names, address, and telephone number.

"We'll get in touch with you as soon as something comes up," the clerk told him.

Frank and Joe got into their car and started for home. As Frank breezed along, Joe suggested:

"Let's drop by Chet's and ask him to get ready. No telling when we may be leaving!"

"Right."

When they slowed down on the road fronting the Morton farm, a strange sight greeted their eyes. In a pasture among a herd of cows rode a cowboy on a chestnut mare.

"Yahoo!" Joe laughed. "It's Chet!"

The boys stopped and got out.

"Hi, pardner!" called Frank. "Where'd you get that rig?"

"Bought it, of course," puffed Chet.

He leaned over in the saddle and looked down at the Hardys. "I'm practicing for our Western trip. Just watch this, fellows!"

Chet swung a rope over his head, then tossed it at a Holstein grazing complacently nearby. The rope snaked through the air and landed over an old tree stump.

"Bull's-eye!" Joe wisecracked.

"That was only the first try," Chet retorted. "Watch this one."

He looped the rope again. It glided through the air and landed neatly over the cow's head.

"How 'bout that!" he cried triumphantly.

Chet, apparently wishing to impress his audience, yanked the rope as he had seen professionals do. With a toss of her head, the animal gave a loud, frightened bellow, then started to run.

Chet had been gazing at Frank and Joe hoping to elicit a word of praise, and was not watching the cow. Suddenly, with a jerk, she pulled him from the horse.

With a thud, somewhat cushioned by his ample weight, the boy landed in a clump of grass. The Hardys roared with laughter.

"Do it again," Joe teased.

He leaned over to help Chet to his feet. As he did so, the cow, tired of the whole annoyance, butted Joe squarely in the rear.

"Oomph!" he grunted as he sprawled in the pasture. The annoyed cow ambled away. Chet enjoyed a few good horselaughs.

"A fine bunch of cowboys you are!" Frank bellowed.

Joe got up and brushed himself off, then looked over at Chet. "Be thankful that wasn't a bull," he said ruefully.

The conversation turned to the boys' latest news. Frank explained the reason for their trip.

"Be ready to fly out West the minute we call you," Joe told Chet. "Dad wants us to start as soon as we can get reservations."

Chet beamed. "Hey, that's swell!"

"And remember, old boy, there's a weight limit on luggage," Frank reminded him.

Chet sighed heavily. "Why, my saddle and boots and duffel bag and—"

"And *you*," Joe teased, "all add up to about five hundred pounds!"

"No fooling," Frank said, "you can't take all this stuff with you."

"I guess you're right," Chet agreed sadly.

"Don't worry." Joe said. "I'm sure they'll have gear for us out at the ranch."

"Boy," Chet exclaimed, "I'd better try to earn some quick money for the trip! I could have helped the farmer down the road build the foundation for his new barn. But there's not time enough!"

"Hop to it," Joe said with a grin. "Do as much as you can." Then he and Frank said good-by and drove off.

Chet did not like to work. But he had no choice. With a sigh that could have been heard all the way to Bayport, he trudged down the road to carry stones for the farmer.

He came home that evening exhausted from the rugged work. The next morning he rose early, put away a man-sized breakfast, and hurried back to his job.

A big truck had dumped a huge pile of stones at the side of the road. It was Chet's chore to haul them in a wheelbarrow to the site of the new foundation. About midday, as he was working alone and figuring on how soon he could get off for a lunchbreak, a strange man approached him.

"Hi," Chet called out, eager for an excuse to rest.

"Looks like you're workin' mighty hard," said the man. He had broad shoulders, a large nose, and bushy black eyebrows.

"Sure am," Chet agreed. "It's tough work, especially when the sun's so hot."

"Well," the stranger replied, "a boy should help his father."

"I'm not doing this for my father," Chet said, leaning against a fence post.

"Oh, no?" asked the man in surprise. "You're just working here?"

"There's a good reason," Chet said as a smile wreathed his round face. "I've got to make some money in a hurry."

"In a hurry?" the man repeated.

"Yes." Chet threw out his chest proudly. "I'm leaving any minute. Goin' out West."

"Is that a fact?" the stranger remarked. "What part of the West?"

Chet was so enthusiastic about his trip that he told the man about the mysterious disappearances at Ruth Hardy's ranch, and how the Hardy boys were taking their father's place to investigate.

A twisted smile, unnoticed by Chet, came to the man's lips as he urged him to go on with his story. When he had finished, the man tugged at the brim of his hat. Then, without another word, he hurried down the road.

"Funny kind of duck," Chet said to himself.

As he watched, the stranger walked under a

low-hanging tree by the side of the road. An instant later Chet heard the roar of a motor and saw a car pull into the road. It sped toward Bayport.

Pondering the man's peculiar actions, Chet sat down to eat his lunch. Suddenly he let out a howl of dismay.

"Oh no," he thought. "I wonder if I told that guy too much!"

He loped home to call his friends.

Meanwhile, the Hardy house was as busy as rodeo day in a prairie town. The airline office had telephoned offering three cancellations to El Paso the following morning. From there the boys would have to charter a plane for the two-hour trip north to Crowhead. After leaving the message with Mrs. Morton, Frank and Joe excitedly began gathering up the things they would need.

During all this time the telephone had been ringing continually. Many friends of the Hardys inquired about the detective's condition. Finally a call came through from Chet.

"Boy, I've been trying to get you guys for an hour!" he complained. "Mother gave me your message about the plane. That's swell. But listen, I think I've pulled a huge boner."

He apologetically told about his talk with the stranger, and described him.

"Wow!" Frank exclaimed. "He sounds like that

bushy-browed man who came to Slow Mo's and tried to take the abandoned car!"

"I shouldn't have opened my big mouth," Chet said.

After hanging up, Frank turned to Joe and told him the story. "That guy is keeping tabs on us," he added. "I don't like it."

The boys had just returned to their packing when the telephone rang again. Aunt Gertrude answered.

"Boys!" she called. "Come here!"

Frank and Joe bounded down the stairs and found her holding a paper.

"A telegram from Ruth," she said, passing her notes over to Frank. He read it aloud:

" *'All is well. No urgency to come to Crow-head. Ruth.'* "

CHAPTER VIII

Followed

FRANK and Joe stared at each other in surprise.

"Oh boy!" Joe exclaimed. "Just when we're all ready to go!"

"I wonder what happened," Frank mused. "Seems like things sure straightened out in a hurry."

"Nothing of the sort," Aunt Gertrude declared emphatically. "I'll bet someone forced her to send this wire!"

"Aunt Gertrude," Joe said with a grin, "you're getting to be more and more like a detective!"

"There's one way to find out for sure," Frank put in. "And that is to telephone Crowhead!" He waited for his aunt's approval, then dialed long-distance. Soon he was connected with the ranch in New Mexico.

"Hello. Cousin Ruth? . . . This is Frank Hardy. Are you all right?"

"Yes, Frank. How are you? And when is your father coming out here?"

"Didn't you just send him a wire saying everything is okay now?"

"Certainly not. The sooner he gets here the better!"

"I'm afraid Dad won't be able to make it, but Joe and I and a friend will arrive sometime tomorrow afternoon," Frank told her. "Dad's ill. We'll tell you all about it when we see you," he added quickly to forestall any questions. Then he said good-by and hung up.

When he told his brother and aunt what Ruth Hardy had said, Joe exclaimed, "She must have an enemy who faked the telegram!"

"Or else the call to our house was phony," Frank suggested. "Let's check the telegraph office."

"Good idea," agreed Joe.

A call to the local wire service proved Frank's surmise to be correct. No telegram had been received from Ruth Hardy.

"Chet's stranger!" Joe cried. "He must have phoned the fake message!"

"Obviously. But why would anyone connected with the Arrow case want to keep us here?" Frank shook his head in puzzlement.

"It doesn't make sense," Joe agreed. "You'd think the thieves would be glad to get us out of town."

Later that afternoon Frank and Joe, accompanied by their aunt, went to the hospital to say good-by to their father. Mr. Hardy was in good spirits, especially since the doctor had told him he could go home within a few days.

"Keep your eyes and ears open," he advised his sons, "and look for the unusual. I'm sure you'll be able to clear up Ruth's troubles."

"We'll do our best, Dad," Frank reassured him.

"Don't take any unnecessary risks," the detective went on. "And keep me posted on what's happening."

When the Hardys, their mother, and Aunt Gertrude reached the airport early the next morning, Chet was already there, sporting a grin and a ten-gallon hat. After good-bys had been said, the three boys boarded the plane.

The big jet taxied out to the runway and soon soared into the sky. Bayport became a mere speck in the distance, finally disappearing on the horizon.

After a smooth flight the craft set down at El Paso, Texas. The boys alighted and went at once to look around for a charter flight to Crowhead. When Frank entered the main terminal a lanky blond stranger approached him.

"You looking for a charter flight?" he asked.

"Yes," Frank replied. "How did you know?"

"Heard you fellows talking when you got off

the plane," the man answered. He looked pleased. "A friend of mine has a nifty ship," he went on. "He'll take you wherever you want to go. And very reasonable."

The stranger's eagerness aroused Frank's suspicions. "I have something to attend to first," he said. "I'll talk to you later if we want to hire your friend."

When Frank told Chet and his brother about the man's offer, they agreed they had better be wary of him.

"He may have followed us from Bayport!" Chet exclaimed.

"Maybe he's mixed up with the phony telegram!" Joe declared.

"Let's look around to see what else is for hire," Frank suggested.

"Not me," Chet put in. "That snack on the plane wasn't enough. I'm going to the restaurant here for some chow."

He went into the airport cafeteria while Frank and Joe strolled off to find a charter flight. About fifteen minutes later Chet had finished a stack of blueberry pancakes when he happened to glance out the window alongside him.

What he saw almost made him choke. There stood the man with the bushy eyebrows to whom he had mentioned the Western trip back on the farm in Bayport! Talking to him was a lanky blond fellow.

"He must be the guy Frank described before," Chet thought. "I've got to tell the Hardys!"

At that moment the Bayport man turned, his eyes meeting Chet's for a split second.

"I don't think he recognized me," Chet told himself and got up.

The men moved on, disappearing around a corner. Chet paid his check and hurried to find Frank and Joe.

They were in front of a hangar, talking to a robust-looking pilot who stood beside a two-engine silver plane. Quickly Chet motioned them aside and told them about the two suspicious strangers.

"I don't like that," Joe replied. "Looks like trouble brewing. We'd better be on our guard at the ranch."

Frank frowned. "There's no doubt we've been followed." Then he turned to the pilot. "Mr. Stratton, I'd like you to meet our friend Chet Morton."

Chet shook hands with the man as Joe said, "Mr. Stratton's a former Air Force pilot. He's agreed to take us all to Crowhead Ranch."

"Terrific!" cried Chet, beaming.

"Welcome aboard," the pilot said affably. "And please—my nickname's Winger. I'll just gas up and check her out, then we'll be ready. Meet you back here in twenty minutes."

During the waiting interval, Frank suggested they check up on Winger, just to be sure they could trust him. A talk with airport officials indicated that the pilot had been flying out of El Paso for years, and was entirely reliable.

"Guess I'm getting too suspicious," Frank admitted, grinning. "But with spies following us—"

"Better safe than sorry, eh?" Joe finished.

At the end of the allotted time, Winger reappeared, directed his passengers to board the plane, and helped with their luggage. Then, taxiing to the end of the runway, he turned, waited for clearance from the tower, headed into the wind and took off smoothly.

"These small planes are great," Joe said enthusiastically.

"Just as safe as the big jets," Frank said confidently.

Chet wished he could agree. He was holding on tightly to the sides of his seat, gazing at the ground below.

"Take your eyes off the scenery," Frank advised, "and look at the clouds!"

Chet turned. Looking backward, he suddenly motioned to the boys excitedly.

"Hey!" he yelled. "I think a plane's following us!"

The pilot turned and agreed. He slowed his roaring engines.

"We'll let him catch up so we can take a closer look. Maybe it's a friend of mine having some fun."

The tailing plane also relaxed its pace, keeping slightly above them.

Frank told Winger just enough of the mystery they were trying to solve to interest him in helping them.

"I'm sure that plane is following us for no good reason," he said.

"Want to change about?" Winger asked.

"What do you mean?"

"I'll get in back of that guy and tail him," Winger said. Then he added, "How's your stomach?"

Frank smiled and Joe answered, "Okay with us. How about you, Chet?"

The boy groaned. The pancakes felt like lead under his belt, but he had no choice but to give the go-ahead sign.

"Get set!" the pilot shouted.

Suddenly the plane shot upward with such velocity that the boys felt as if they were being pressed into their seats by an invisible hand.

In a breath-taking swoop, the craft was upside down at the top of a tight inside loop. Then it dived down directly in back of their mysterious pursuers!

CHAPTER IX

Forced Landing

Taken by surprise, the pilot of the mystery plane tried to shake off Winger's ship. He banked first to the right, then to the left. But the former Air Force man stuck to his quarry.

"Atta boy!" Joe cried gleefully, admiring their pilot's deft maneuvering.

Chet did not say a word. His eyes stared straight ahead as if glued to a specter.

Finally the kibitzing plane, after zooming in vain to get away from Winger's craft, headed back toward El Paso. Winger followed. The pursued ship headed directly for the airport and descended.

Winger remained aloft for a few minutes. He had to wait for landing permission from the tower. The boys watched as their quarry landed. But suddenly they gasped. The craft had hardly touched down on the runway when it made a daring take-off!

"Follow him!" Joe cried out.

"I can't," the pilot replied. He had just received orders to come in. "Against regulations to go up without checking in," he added.

"But that fellow didn't," Joe said.

"I know. Let's see what the airport people know about him."

Chet remained in the plane, while Winger and the Hardys went to the terminal. They found a group of angry officials discussing the mysterious plane which had broken the rules of the field. It had come in without a signal and taken off without reporting.

No one had been close enough to see its registration number. It had swooped in and out too quickly.

Frank related the story of their experience. They could offer little to identify the plane, except that it was a white two-engine craft and appeared to be carrying two men. The officials promised to do what they could to trace the lawbreakers.

"Well, let's start all over again," Winger proposed as they walked back to their craft.

"I hope Chet hasn't run off." Joe grinned. "I don't think he and his pancakes liked your little stunt, Winger."

But Chet was in the seat where they had left him.

"How do you feel?" Winger asked him.

Chet bobbed his head up and down, saying nothing.

A few minutes later they were in the air again. Here and there dense woodlands dotted the hills and cattle country. Once in a while a picturesque ranch house came into view below.

"According to your directions, we should be headed straight for Crowhead," Winger said an hour later. "Ever been there before by air?"

"No," Frank replied. "But we have a good idea of the layout."

"Well, when you recognize anything, give a shout."

Frank and Joe alertly watched the terrain beneath them. Presently the plane droned over a strand of ponderosa pines.

Frank, glancing from the right side of the craft, suddenly reached out and grabbed Joe's arm.

"Hey, look at that!"

"What is it?" Winger queried, while Joe and Chet jumped up and looked out Frank's window.

"There among the trees," Frank pointed.

"I see it!" Joe exclaimed. "It's a giant arrow cut out of the woods!"

"A crooked arrow!" Chet observed.

Winger was puzzled. "What on earth could that mean?" he asked. He banked to go back and look at the strange sight again.

"It looks," said Frank, "as if the timber has been cut purposely in the form of a bent arrow.

Let's circle around to see if we can spot anything else."

"Okay with me," the pilot agreed.

Winger flew in ever-widening circles. But the dense woodland yielded no signs of habitation and no further markers.

Finally the pilot came back again to the crooked arrow. Frank nudged Joe, who bent his head closer to his brother.

"Do you see where the arrow points?" he whispered excitedly.

"Right toward Crowhead Ranch!" Joe replied. The two exchanged significant glances.

"I wonder what it all means," Joe said, puzzled.

"You've got me," Frank remarked with concern. "But this, together with the phony telegram, seems to prove there is a connection between this area and the gang of thieves. We'll have to find out what it is, and pronto!"

"I wish we could see if anybody's down there," Joe said. "It might be a hideout for the gang!"

"No chance of landing among these trees," Frank declared.

As the pilot headed away from the arrow, Joe noticed a cleared spot beyond the arrow's head. He was about to bring it to Winger's attention when suddenly the airplane's engines began to sputter. Winger looked back at the boys, his forehead wrinkled with concern.

"It's a giant arrow!" Joe exclaimed

"I may have to take her down!" he called grimly.

"Crowhead's not far from here," Frank said.

"There's a field to our left," Joe put in. "Maybe we could land there if we have to."

Winger tried frantically to get the proper response from the engines, but they continued to wheeze and cough.

"Down we go!" he yelled.

The wind whined against the plane's surface as the craft, under Winger's steady hand, made for the clearing. Chet closed his eyes in terror, but the Hardys, fascinated by the pilot's skill, watched every move.

The plane banked, its wings brushing the tree-tops. At last it settled down in the field without mishap.

"Whew!" Chet cried out. "That was too close for comfort!"

"Sure was," Winger agreed. "I just hope we can get out of here again."

They all jumped from the plane. Frank, who was a good mechanic, offered to help examine the engines for the trouble spot.

Before he went to work, he said to Chet and Joe, "How about you two taking a look around to see if you can find out anything about that arrow?"

"Okay," Joe said, ready for adventure.

Chet stared at the unknown, and to him, hostile

surroundings. He felt no great desire to move one foot.

"A walk will do you good," Joe urged.

Chet remained where he was. "I knew it," he complained. "I come out West for a good time, and the next thing I know I'm in a gangsters' hideout!"

"That shouldn't bother you. How about that judo you learned?" Joe needled him. "You could throw a couple of gunmen right over your shoulder."

"Gunmen?" Chet's eyebrows shot up. "That settles it. I'll help on the engine. You and Frank go."

It took quite a bit of persuasion on the Hardys' part before Chet finally set off with Joe. Cautiously they advanced among the trees, but there was no sign of human habitation.

It was evident, however, that someone had been there recently because the land in the crooked arrow area had been stripped of all new growth so that the arrow sign could be plainly seen from the air.

"This spot must be here to mark that clearing we used as an airstrip," Joe concluded. "Probably for members of the crooked arrow gang. That may have been their white plane following us!"

The boys hunted for clues to the criminals' identity but found nothing. Finally they returned to the plane. Winger and Frank had located the trouble. There was water in one of the fuel tanks.

"We think someone tampered with the plane," Frank reported gravely. "Winger says a couple of guys were hanging around while he was getting gas and checking her out."

"Those two I saw talking!" Chet exclaimed.

"Then we're lucky to be safe!" Joe cried out.

"Did you fellows find anything?" Frank inquired.

"No," Joe reported, "but from the cuts on the stumps, it's a safe bet those trees were felled on purpose."

"Whoever did it surely went to a lot of trouble," commented Winger as he tightened a coupling in the fuel line. "Maybe it's a landing field, but the pilot would have to be pretty good to get in and out of here!"

A few minutes later he added, "We're ready to go. The really tough job is ahead—to take off!" He eyed the length of the clearing. "Well, I guess we can make it," he said. "But I wish we could throw off some excess weight."

Joe eyed Chet slyly.

"Oh, no, you don't!" the stout boy protested with a broad grin.

They climbed back into the plane, and Winger took his place at the controls. He taxied to the end of the clearing and turned, taking advantage of every inch of ground. He applied the brakes until the engines roared, then zipped down the natural runway.

The boys held their breath as the plane sped toward the trees at the far end of the open space. Suddenly, with a bound like a high jumper, the craft nosed up sharply. Boughs scratched the underside of the fuselage, but the ship soared into the sky unscathed. Winger was perspiring as he leveled off.

"That was great," Frank praised him, and the others added their congratulations.

It was late afternoon when the plane landed at Crowhead. Frank had identified the ranch from the layout of the buildings, and Winger set the wheels down on a big field alongside the house.

Chet eyed his surroundings with suspicion, but everything seemed to be peaceful. Several cowhands came to the plane. After greetings and introductions were made, the men helped unload the luggage and two of them took it into the house. The boys paid Winger, thanked him, and said good-by.

Two other cowhands escorted the boys to a wide vine-covered porch encircling three sides of the large ranch house. Cousin Ruth was there at the door and greeted them warmly.

"It's a shame about your father," she said, "but I'm grateful to you for coming out here to help me."

The boys introduced Chet to their cousin, who had changed considerably since they had last seen her. Her hair, once blond, was now streaked with gray, and her face was careworn from the ordeal of her husband's death and the responsibilities of the ranch.

After the visitors had brought Cousin Ruth up to date on the news from home, she showed them to two comfortably furnished bedrooms. Then they were treated to a sumptuous Western meal. Chet was in his glory.

"Golly," he cried, seeing the platter of juicy charcoaled steaks, "Bayport was never like this!"

When the meal was over, the boys excused themselves and walked around the ranch. It was not until dusk had fallen that Ruth Hardy joined them again and broached the subject they were so eager to hear.

They had gathered in the attractive, dark-beamed living room with its massive rough-stone fireplace. The widow closed the door, glanced furtively out the window, then launched into the story of the difficulties at Crowhead. The boys leaned forward attentively.

"One by one my best cowhands have been disappearing," she began. "They leave very suddenly, taking all their belongings with them."

"And don't they tell you they're going?" Frank asked.

"They tell no one. As a result, my foreman

hasn't been able to get all the ranch work done."

"Can't you hire new hands?" Joe spoke up.

"They won't work here. We've advertised, but the story has gotten around that Crowhead is—well—jinxed. Because nobody has heard from the men who disappear."

"What do the police say?" Joe asked.

"The sheriff has done all he can to try to solve the mystery, but the men keep vanishing into thin air."

As their cousin talked, night dropped into the valley. She switched on the living-room lights and said, "You boys must be exhausted. Perhaps you had better go to bed. We get up very early here at Crowhead."

"And I'd like to do some investigating in the morning," Frank declared. "How about it, fellows?"

As he rose from his chair he happened to glance out the window. A pair of unfriendly eyes was peering into the room. Then, almost instantly, the image vanished.

CHAPTER X

A Suspicious Foreman

"Somebody is spying on us!" Frank thought.

He sidled over to the window, but whoever had been peering through it had disappeared from view. Excusing himself, Frank went into the kitchen and out the back door, hoping to take the spy by surprise.

He made his way quietly around the building. Nobody was near the window, and it was too dark to check for footprints.

As Frank listened for a noise to indicate the eavesdropper's whereabouts, he heard the sound of hoofbeats. They came from the direction of the corral, then rumbled off in the distance like the muffled beat of a drum.

"He sure got away in a hurry," Frank thought in disgust.

When he went inside, his cousin asked him

what had happened. Not wishing to worry her, he merely said he was investigating a noise he had heard.

Frank kept his discovery secret until he and Joe were alone in their room. Chet had already tumbled into bed and was sleeping soundly.

"We'd better not alarm Cousin Ruth," Frank said when he had completed his story. "But there's something I'd like to ask her before we turn in. Be right back."

Seeing a light still on in the living room, he went to find his cousin. She was reading.

"Oh," she said in surprise, "would you boys like a snack or something? I forgot to ask."

"No, thank you," Frank replied. "Joe and I were just wondering exactly how many horses are in the corral."

"We have twenty-five now," Mrs. Hardy said, a note of sadness in her voice. "We used to have many more, but I had to sell them."

After chatting a while longer, Frank said good night again and went to his room. He suggested a plan to Joe.

Instead of undressing, the Hardys turned out their light and waited. A few minutes later their cousin went to her bedroom. Half an hour later Crowhead Ranch was cloaked in stillness, broken only by the chirping of crickets and the occasional mournful howl of a far-off coyote.

"Okay," Frank whispered. "Let's go!"

The boys tiptoed downstairs to the kitchen, opened the back door, and made their way to the corral. The horses stirred slightly as they sensed the presence of strangers.

"Hope they don't rouse anybody," Frank said.

Just then the moon, whose ghostly light had been concealed behind a mass of somber clouds, broke into the open sky. In the dim glow cast over the corral, Frank and Joe could see the horses.

"We'll both count them," Frank said.

After a moment of silence, Joe whispered, "Twenty-four!"

"That's what I get!" Frank replied.

"There's one missing," Joe said excitedly.

"That might mean," Frank declared, "that the person who looked in the window and rode off works for Crowhead!"

"Listen!" Joe warned suddenly.

The boys held their breath.

"I hear it!" Frank said hoarsely. "It's a rider. Maybe the same one coming back!"

They raced into the shadow of a shed which stood near the corral, and waited. The hoofbeats grew closer. A few minutes later a cowboy reined in his mount at the corral gate and dismounted. After quickly unsaddling, he lifted the bar, slapped his horse on the rump, and the animal bounded inside.

All the while Frank and Joe craned their necks

to get a glimpse of the man. But the dark shadow thrown by his broad-brimmed hat concealed his face.

The boys noted that he was tall and rangy, but so were many other cowboys. If only they could get a good look at him!

The man hastened toward the bunkhouse. As he neared the Hardys' hiding place, Frank and Joe flattened themselves against the side of the building. Their hearts beat like trip-hammers.

When the cowboy passed them, he suddenly whipped off his hat and wiped his brow with the back of his wrist. The moon shone full on a stern face with a thin nose and jutting jaw.

He hurried on, and soon the boys heard the bunkhouse door shut lightly after him. When all was quiet again, they made their way silently to the house.

"We'll spot him in the morning," Frank whispered. "Something's up!"

They opened the back door, which they had left ajar. Then, taking off their shoes, they crept back up to their room.

In the morning the brothers were awakened by a brilliant sunrise.

"Swell country," Joe commented.

"Sure is. We've got to see to it that Cousin Ruth doesn't lose this ranch," Frank declared.

The Hardys roused Chet, who rolled sleepily from bed.

"Hi, it's time to get up," Joe said as he prodded his friend.

"Lemme sleep," Chet protested.

"You're going to miss breakfast," Frank teased. "They don't serve it in bed, you know."

At the mention of food, the stocky boy quickly shook off his drowsiness and dressed. Ruth Hardy greeted them in the living room.

"Breakfast isn't quite ready yet," she said. "Suppose we go outside and I'll introduce you to the men."

They stepped onto the rambling porch, then walked toward the bunkhouse. A group of cowboys, some of whom the Easterners had not seen the day before, were getting ready for their day's work.

"I'd like you to meet my two cousins Frank and Joe and their friend Chet," the widow said pleasantly, approaching the cowboys. "They're from Bayport and are spending a little vacation with us."

"Howdy," said the men, shaking hands with the trio.

Ruth Hardy introduced them one by one. Presently she stopped beside a little fellow with shiny black hair. His leathery face was as weather-beaten as a mountain rock, but the crinkly expression around his eyes indicated a keen sense of humor.

"I know you'll like Crowhead's Pye," their cousin said, turning to the boys.

"Pie?" Chet returned enthusiastically. "For breakfast?"

A few of the cowboys laughed.

"No." Mrs. Hardy smiled. "This is Pye. P-y-e. His real name is Pymatuno, and he's the best Indian cowhand in all of New Mexico!" Then she looked around, as if she had missed somebody.

"Where's Hank?" she asked. Turning to her visitors, she explained, "He's my foreman."

As she spoke, the bunkhouse door slammed and a tall man emerged. The Hardys stared in amazement. He had a thin nose and jutting jaw—the same as the mysterious rider of the night before.

When he approached the group, Ruth Hardy introduced him.

"Howdy," he said, extending a long, bony hand and showing no enthusiasm at the meeting. "Up purty early for city kids, ain't yo'?" He looked at the trio with a poker face.

The boys resented the remark, especially Joe, who was not endowed with the same even temper as his older brother.

"It seems to me," he said pointedly, "that certain cowboys stay out at night as late as city folks!"

Hank tensed. The muscles on his lean cheeks bulged in and out.

"Sometimes," he snapped, "a cowboy has to run off coyotes."

Just then the mellow strum of a guitar was heard. A pint-sized cowboy, wearing a bright-red shirt, walked from the bunkhouse.

"That's Terry," Ruth Hardy said with a smile. "He's a lot of fun, but an awful tease."

"He's mighty fleet-fingered with the gee-tar," one of the men spoke up.

The singing cowboy grinned, showing a set of white teeth. He strummed a few chords, greeted the visitors from Bayport, then broke into song.

> 'Ef yo' wanna be a cowman
> Yo' gotta find a frisky hoss
> In this rough-and-tumble land,
> And ride to beat the band.

> "But take a soft old city lad
> Ah, how his hoss will fuss
> It sure will be a pity
> When his rider hits the dust!"

Terry gaily twanged out an extra chord as the group roared with laughter.

At that moment the ranch-house bell rang. Ruth Hardy and the somewhat embarrassed "city kids" went off to breakfast. When they had finished the hearty meal of flapjacks and sausage, they lingered at the table.

Finally Frank addressed his cousin. "You know," he said, "I don't mind being razzed because I'm from the city, but it seemed to me that your foreman Hank wasn't kidding. Is he always like that?"

"Oh, Hank's all right," Ruth Hardy assured the boys. "He's a little dictatorial, but I think he means well."

"Seems mighty unfriendly to me," Joe said with a worried frown. "Maybe your men are leaving on account of him."

"I hardly think so. Hank just doesn't like what he calls 'city dudes.' I'm sure you can grow to be friends, though."

"I hope so," Frank said. But he was still suspicious that the foreman might be mixed up in some way with the strange disappearance of the Crowhead cowboys.

Soon their cousin excused herself from the table and the boys continued the discussion.

"You know," Frank began, "no matter how confident Cousin Ruth is about her foreman, I think we'd better keep our eye on him."

"Right," Joe agreed. "Let's get started looking for clues."

Chet swallowed hard. "If you're going anywhere on horseback, I think I'll take a rain check. Guess I ate too much Western breakfast."

Frank and Joe let out a hearty laugh.

"Okay, dude," Joe quipped. "Meet you back here after we take a look around Crowhead."

The Hardys walked to the corral, eager to ride over the meandering acres of the ranch. When they asked the foreman for horses, Hank lifted the corral bar and went inside. He returned with two lively mounts.

"Saddle 'em yoreselves," he said gruffly.

The animals pranced and pawed, but finally the boys got the saddles strapped in place. Hank looked on amazed as they swung themselves easily onto the horses' backs.

At that moment a figure raced toward them. It was Pye.

"Get off!" he shouted excitedly. "They're bad horses!"

Hank glared at the Indian. "Stay out o' this!" he ordered.

As he spoke, Joe's horse reared. The next instant the mount did a sunfish, tossing Joe off his back into the dust!

CHAPTER XI

A Second Chance

HANK guffawed at Joe's bad spill but made no attempt to subdue the rearing horse.

It was Pye who rushed in and grabbed the animal's bridle, yanking him away from the boy.

Frank had dismounted and rushed to his brother. But Joe picked himself up and brushed the dirt from his jeans.

Hank's laughter suddenly turned into an angry frown as he saw Terry, the singing cowboy, approaching with two other horses.

"Who told yo' to bring 'em?" he shouted.

The little cowboy grinned, at the same time letting forth in a high tenor voice:

> *"Yo' can't ride a bronc*
> *The very first day.*
> *Yippee-aye-o,*
> *Yippe-aye-yay!"*

"Shut up!" Hank bellowed. "Yo're not gettin' paid for singin'."

"I'm only tryin' to make the boys feel at home," Terry said.

"Leave that to Mrs. Hardy," the foreman declared. He turned to Pye, who had led the horses back into the corral.

"Look here!" he snapped. "Get those tenderfeet to work ridin' fence!"

"Yes, sir!" Pye grinned.

The foreman strode off, leaving the boys with the Indian. He offered to saddle the new mounts, but Frank and Joe cinched their own. Then Pye mounted a little pinto and the three started for the fences.

"Hey, you're pretty good riders," Pye said, surprised at the ease with which the Hardys handled their mounts.

"We've done some riding back home," Frank replied.

"Nice pinto you've got there, Pye," Joe said admiringly. Pye and his horse moved in perfect rhythm.

"He's a fine horse," the Indian said proudly. "And he knows two languages—English and Navaho."

With that he spoke an Indian word. The pinto stopped and dropped to his forelegs. Then Pye spoke in English and the pony rose.

Pye looked at the boys gleefully. "See?" he said.

"That pony's smart. And he never went to school, either."

The boys laughed. "What's his name?" Frank asked as they cantered along.

"Cherry," the Indian replied. "The cowboys make fun of me sometimes. Call me and my horse Cherry Pye." He grinned until his eyes almost disappeared.

The country over which the three rode was rough and scrubby. Here and there a few cattle grazed on the green patches dotting the terrain.

Pye's admiration of the boys' horsemanship was unbounded. Finding that they showed no signs of fatigue, he urged them toward the northern fence line of the ranch.

"Nice up there," he said. "A long time ago Indians used to live up that way."

As they neared the boundary, Frank thought he heard the distant hum of a motor. He called his brother's attention to it.

"Sounds like a plane," Joe remarked, scanning the sky.

They realized that occasionally a transport might pass over the area, flying at a very high altitude. But this one was low.

"There it is," Pye declared, pointing over a wooded section a few miles ahead of them. A small white plane suddenly appeared and skimmed over the treetops.

"Joe!" Frank cried. "Isn't that the same one—?"

"Sure looks like it," Joe put in. "The one that followed us from El Paso yesterday!"

Pye regarded them curiously. "I've seen that plane many times," he said finally. "It always flies low over those trees."

Frank and Joe exchanged glances. Was it in some way connected with the mystery at Crowhead?

Suddenly Joe reined in sharply. "Look, Frank!" he cried excitedly. "The plane's coming down!"

The three watched as the craft banked and disappeared behind the trees.

"Do you suppose it's in trouble?" Joe asked his brother.

"Could be," Frank replied. "But it looked to me as if the pilot meant to land."

"Let's find out," Joe declared.

But hardly were the words out of his mouth when the plane zoomed sharply into the air.

"It didn't land after all," Joe commented. "What do you make of that?"

"Maybe he's just having fun," Pye suggested with a grin.

"Why would a pilot fool around out here?" Frank queried. "He'd be in serious trouble if he crashed. This country is too wooded to try any hopping."

As the plane flew off, Frank spotted something

in the cockpit that confirmed his belief the pilot was not on a playful junket. The sun's rays were reflected in the lenses of what was probably a pair of binoculars!

Joe saw it at the same time. "He's looking for something, Frank."

"And that something may be *us*," his brother replied with a frown.

By this time the trio were close to the woods. Pye hesitated, asking if the Hardys wanted to ride into it. Eager to learn where the pilot had planned to come down, they nodded.

As they entered the dark stillness, Frank felt a peculiar sensation. The trees, although not the tallest he had seen, appeared to stretch their limbs grotesquely toward the riders. Their gnarled branches, disfigured by wind and storm, seemed to beckon the boys into a trap which nature itself had devised.

"This sure is a spooky place," Joe remarked.

"Very bad," Pye said. "Cowboys sometimes get lost in here. But I know my way around pretty well."

Buoyed by the Indian's confidence, the boys entered the woods, ducking low-hanging branches along a faintly marked trail. Suddenly the pinto whinnied and stopped.

"Someone's coming!" Pye warned.

The three dismounted, leading their animals off the trail. As they did, a young cowboy, panting as if he had run for miles, came stumbling along the path. A sudden look of recognition came over the Indian's face.

"Pete!" he shouted at the tall, redheaded youth.

The runner was apparently one of the men from Crowhead. He stopped, a wild look in his eyes.

"Where are you going?" Frank asked him.

"Ch-chasin' my pony," Pete replied. "He—er —ran away."

"We didn't see him," Pye said. "He didn't come this way."

"Here," Frank offered, "climb up and ride back of me. We'll take you back to the ranch. It's a long way."

"No," the redhead replied. His shifting eyes looked right and left into the woods. "I'll keep on lookin' for him."

With that he started off again along the trail and disappeared into the woods.

"I'm going to follow him," Frank said presently. "This looks mighty suspicious."

"Pye and I'll stay here awhile and see if anyone else comes along," Joe said. "Pete may have been running to meet somebody."

Frank wheeled his horse around and headed after the disappearing Pete. When he was out of sight of Joe and Pye, Frank glanced around, hoping to pick up some clue to Pete's strange behavior. What he saw sent a quiver of excitement racing down his spine.

At the base of a nearby pine tree lay a large, smooth rock. Carved on its face was a crooked arrow!

Frank bent low in his saddle to get a better look at it. As he did so, an object whizzed past him. It sounded like the buzz of a giant bee.

An instant later something sang closer to the boy's head. It was followed by a zinging thud. An arrow had embedded itself in a tree trunk directly in front of him!

Another loud zing! Frank fell to the ground!

CHAPTER XII

Bunkhouse Brawl

FRANK lay motionless. The whizzing arrow had barely missed his shoulder. He remained flattened to the ground to make himself as inconspicuous a target as possible for his unseen assailant.

Minutes went by. There were no more shots. Frank raised his head slightly to look through the brush.

Not ten feet away lay a short arrow. Near its nock were three white feathers.

"The same kind of arrow that injured Dad!" Frank thought in amazement.

He pulled himself along the ground and grasped the shaft. No doubt of it. This arrow was a duplicate of the one that had wounded his dad. Perhaps it had come from the same quiver! Had the archer traveled from Bayport to New Mexico?

Cautiously Frank arose and looked around. He saw no one. Then he wrapped the weapon in his kerchief and tied it to his saddle.

Frank spotted another arrow embedded in a tree a few yards away. From its position, he figured approximately the point from which the missile had been shot.

Keeping his eyes open for any movement among the trees, Frank skirted the direct line of attack and approached the place from the rear. But when he reached the small clearing where the assailant must have stood, it was deserted.

As he returned to his horse, Frank mulled over the strange turn of events. The giant crooked arrow cut in the timber, the crooked arrow chipped into the rock, and the white-feathered shafts seemed to fit into the same eerie pattern. But the mystery remained as deep as the woods in which Frank stood.

His thoughts were suddenly interrupted by the sounds of crackling twigs and hoofbeats. Perhaps Pete was returning. Or even the mysterious archer!

Frank quickly led his horse into a gully, then dived into a tangle of underbrush to wait.

To his relief, he saw Joe and Pye emerge from among the trees. Frank startled them when he sidled into their path.

"You're stealthy as an Indian," Pye said, grinning.

"You'd be quiet too," Frank replied, "if somebody had been taking potshots at you with a bow and arrow!"

Joe and the cowboy looked puzzled as Frank told his story.

"Nobody at Crowhead uses arrows," Pye said, frowning.

"Is there an Indian reservation near here?" Frank queried.

For a moment the man was thoughtful. "No," he said finally. "The nearest one is over a hundred miles away."

"Then there wouldn't be any Indians wandering around these woods," Joe reasoned.

Frank nodded. "Let's go back to the place where I was attacked," he suggested, and led the way to the stone into which the crooked arrow symbol had been cut. He watched Pye's expression intently. It reflected utter amazement, just as Joe's.

"Ever see anything like this before?" Frank asked.

Pye shook his head. "Never. Indians don't make crooked arrows, never have. White men might!"

"What do you mean?"

The cowboy shrugged. "You seem to think that arrows are exclusively used by Indians. It just isn't so. It's true that they were our only weapons a long time ago, but not crooked ones like this!"

"I guess you're right," Frank said.

After the analysis of the wrist-watch strap, they had assumed that an Indian was involved. But perhaps the archer was a white man trying to mislead the Hardys into thinking Indians were the culprits!

"Let's have some food and turn back," said Pye. "It's a long ride."

After eating the sandwiches they had packed in their saddlebags, and drinking water from their canteens, the three headed home. There was little conversation on the way. After several hot, tedious hours on horseback, they reached the inviting coolness of the shaded ranch.

Frank went straight to the bunkhouse to find Hank. The foreman eyed the boy suspiciously.

"What's the matter now?" he asked. "Yo' got good horses, didn't yo'?"

"I'm looking for Pete," Frank said, ignoring the question. "Did he get back? We saw him in the woods some time ago. Said he had lost his horse and was looking for it."

"Pete's been gone since early morning," Hank scowled. "Now don't bother me again."

Later, as the boys enjoyed a hearty meal of pot roast and oven-browned potatoes, they chatted with Chet and Cousin Ruth about the details of the day's adventures.

The evening wore on, and still Pete had not returned. Frank and Joe learned that the cowboy's horse had trotted back, but without a saddle.

Ruth Hardy was very upset. Pete was one of her best hands. According to the other men, he

had seemed happy at Crowhead. "I can't understand it," she said to Frank. "You see what hap-
pens? One day a cowboy is here, the next he's
gone—with no explanation."

Frank was eager to report to his father, and put
in the call to home. When Mr. Hardy answered,
his voice sounded strong and clear. He said he was
feeling better and asked how things were at Crowhead.

Frank and Joe took turns in relating the
mysterious happenings. When Frank told of the
crooked arrow marker cut in the timber, and
the sign carved in the stone, the boy could sense
that his father was astonished.

"Did that arrow and the one you saw from the
air point in the same direction?" he asked.

"Yes, Dad," Frank replied.

"Then keep looking for more clues in those
woods. But be careful, and don't go far without
someone trustworthy from Crowhead."

"Right."

After the boys had finished their story, Mr.
Hardy brought them up to date on the mystery
from the Bayport angle. The car in Slow Mo's
garage was still unclaimed. Tobacco Shop Jenk
remained silent. No more telltale wrist watches
had been located. But the police lab had found
that the Arrow cigarettes contained a methane
derivative which was highly toxic.

"Sam Radley and government agents," Mr.

Hardy said, "have arrested several peddlers of Arrow cigarettes in the Bayport area and in other sections of the country. But they haven't yet nabbed the ringleader."

"Maybe he's Arrow Charlie," Frank suggested.

"We have a trap set for him if he shows up here," the detective said. "But he may show up out there. Watch your step!"

The boys promised they would, and the conversation ended. Frank, Joe, and Chet spent the rest of the evening near the corral and the bunkhouse but learned nothing. No riders came in or went out and Pete did not return. Finally at midnight they decided to go to bed.

They were up early the next morning. Frank and Joe noticed that Chet did not eat his usual heavy breakfast.

"What's the matter, Chet?" Joe needled as the Hardys were about to leave the table. "Lost your Eastern appetite?"

"No more third helpings for me," the boy declared.

Frank grinned. "Aren't you afraid of starving to death?"

"No," Chet declared sheepishly. "I'm afraid of feeling too full to ride, and missing out on all the fun!"

Nevertheless, he finished his second stack of flapjacks before he joined his friends in a stroll around the ranch buildings. As they neared the bunkhouse, a cheerful voice called out the door-way.

"Mornin'. Come in. I got somethin' to show yo'."

It was Terry. He held the door open for them to enter.

"There 'tis," he said, pointing.

A long pine table stood in the middle of the cowboys' quarters. On it lay three piles of range riding clothes.

"Some o' the men kinda got an apology to make," he said. "Leastways to Frank an' Joe. We found out from Pye yo' sure can ride. So a few of us got together some gear for yo'."

"That was mighty nice!" Frank exclaimed. "Thanks."

"Swell of you," Joe cried, examining the bright shirts and bandannas.

"We had a little trouble gettin' pants to fit yore friend here." Terry smiled, glancing at Chet.

The boys got into their new outfits enthusiastically. Chet pulled a wide-brimmed hat rakishly to the side of his head.

"Gimme my six-shooters!" he cried, spreading his feet wide apart and slapping his hips. *"Ya-hoo!"*

The cowboys hooted, and the visitors thanked Terry for his pals' generosity, adding they had not expected such treatment from Hank.

"Hank don't know about this," Terry replied,

"or his pals Muff and Jed. Just keep it under yore hat, will yo'? Better go. Here comes Hank now."

Chet and the Hardys hastily departed from the bunkhouse. Nearing the corral, Chet suddenly wheeled around.

"Gosh, I forgot my bandanna!" he exclaimed.

He hotfooted back to the bunkhouse. Terry had gone. The bandanna lay on the floor beside the table.

As Chet leaned down to pick it up he heard Hank's voice. The foreman was talking on a telephone in an alcove of the bunkhouse. Chet could not help but overhear the conversation.

"Not till those guys from Bayport leave," the dour cowboy said.

He hung up and turned to go out. Seeing Chet approaching the door, Hank became furious.

"What yo' doin' sneakin' in here?"

"I c-came for my bandanna," Chet stammered.

"Likely story," Hank snarled. "Yo're eaves-droppin'!"

This was too much for Chet. "What were you saying about us?" he demanded hotly.

"None o' yore business!" Hank barked.

He strode toward Chet and grabbed him by the shirt front. Twisting his fist, he lifted him nearly off the floor.

Suddenly Chet remembered the armlock grip that Russ Griggs had taught him. With a quick movement, he grasped Hank's left wrist with his right hand. The foreman, caught off balance, relaxed his hold on Chet's shirt.

With another lightninglike move, Chet thrust his left hand under Hank's shoulder, using it as a fulcrum. An agonizing look of pain came over Hank's face as Chet bent his arm back. With a flip, Chet hurled the man across the room. Hank teetered backward on his heels, then crashed onto a cot in the corner of the bunkhouse.

Hank quickly regained his feet, roaring, "I'll throw yo' blasted nuisances off this place!"

Just then two hulking cowboys strode into the building.

"Muff! Jed! Grab that guy!" Hank ordered, pointing to Chet.

Hank's friends advanced on Chet, pinning his arms to his sides.

"What'll we do with him?" one of them asked.

"Tie him to a steer's tail!" Hank thundered.

CHAPTER XIII

A Poisoned Point

"Lemme go!" Chet cried. "Help! Frank! Joe!"

"Shut up, blubberhead!" Hank growled.

Suddenly the door of the bunkhouse burst open. Frank and Joe rushed in, followed by Terry.

"What's going on here?" Frank shouted as he saw his friend held captive by the two burly cowhands.

Hank wheeled around. "Yo' stay out o' this!" he snapped. "This is between me and yore fat friend!"

"Leave him alone, Boss," Terry pleaded.

"Mind yore own business." The foreman glowered. "These kids got no right in the bunkhouse."

"Yeah!" growled Muff. "Let's throw them out!"

Muff's right hand lashed out at Frank. But before it could find its mark, the boy grasped his wrist in a viselike hold.

In a split second the place was in an uproar.

109

Hank rushed at Joe. As Jed unloosed his hold on the stout boy, Chet tangled with him.

Arms and legs flew as the Hardys and Chet put their judo lessons to practical use.

Moments later, Hank was draped over a cot. The other two sat on the floor, reclining on their elbows, their legs stretched out V-shaped in front of them.

"A mighty funny sight," drawled Terry.

Hank and his friends pulled themselves to their feet and limped toward the back door of the bunkhouse. As Hank left, he turned around and pointed a finger at the boys.

"I'll get yo' for this!" he muttered. "I'm boss around here!"

Terry looked worried. "Hank's a bad actor when he's got a grudge," he said. "Be careful."

Suddenly the singing cowboy's mood changed. He reached for his guitar and broke into a broad smile. "Listen to this." He grinned, struck a few chords, then raised his head and burst out:

> *"Thar was a city slicker*
> *Dared fight with foreman Hank.*
> *Now the city kid was quicker.*
> *He had his wits to thank.*

> *"So foreman Hank went flyin'*
> *Right clean through the air.*
> *I'll remember till I'm dyin'*
> *His sad look of despair."*

"A mighty funny sight!" drawled Terry

"Swell!" Joe exclaimed, laughing. "Only better not let Hank hear it!"

Terry nodded and said that it was time he started on his chores. The boys walked as far as the corral gate with him, then went toward the house.

"That sure was nice going, Chet," Frank said, slapping his pal on the back. "Maybe Hank won't bother us for a while."

"What started the whole mess, anyway?" Joe asked.

Chet told about the telephone conversation he had overheard. Frank and Joe scowled.

"Wonder what it is he can't do while we're around," Frank remarked grimly.

"There's sure something fishy going on," commented Joe.

"You don't have to remind me, especially after yesterday's adventure," Frank said. "By the way, we ought to track down that clue."

"Which clue?" Joe asked.

"The arrow," Frank replied. "The one that nearly hit me in the woods!"

"What are you going to do with it?" Chet asked.

"I think we should take a close look at the tip," Frank replied. "Come on. Now's as good a time as any."

Joe and Chet followed him to the brothers' room where Frank had cached the white-feathered arrow. He dipped the tip in a saucer of water for a few seconds, then carefully carried the saucer down onto the porch.

A fly buzzed around the water, then settled down to investigate. When it touched the liquid, the insect struggled briefly and died.

"Just as I thought!" Frank declared. "Poison! But to make sure, let's take the arrow to Santa Fe and have it analyzed."

Frank told Cousin Ruth what he had in mind, then put in a long-distance call to the young pilot who had flown them to Crowhead. Winger happened to be free and promised to come for them at once.

At noon the drone of a plane was heard over the ranch. Winger landed alongside the house and the boys walked over to meet him.

Frank got in, carrying the arrow wrapped in waxed paper. His brother and Chet followed.

Hank saw them from a distance. A queer smile tugged at the corners of his hard mouth.

"There they go," he drawled to a cowboy standing nearby. "I hope for good!"

When the boys landed in Santa Fe they went directly to a chemist recommended by Ruth Hardy. Frank asked him to analyze the arrow tip.

"I'll have the report ready in about an hour," the chemist said, "if you care to come back."

"Sure will."

The boys left the arrow and strolled down the street.

"How about some lunch?" Joe suggested.

"Best idea yet," Chet agreed. "I'm starved."

They saw a drugstore nearby and went in. On a chance, Frank went over to the man behind the prescription counter and asked in a low voice:

"Have you any Arrow cigarettes?"

The druggist looked quizzically at the boy. "Arrow cigarettes?" he echoed. "Never heard of them."

Frank, feeling the man was telling the truth, rejoined the others at the soda fountain. After the boys had finished eating, they paid their bill and returned to the laboratory.

When the chemist appeared, Frank hurried over to him. "What did you find?" he asked excitedly.

' This arrowhead is poisoned," the man replied gravely. "Had the arrow penetrated the skin it might have proved fatal!"

Frank paid the man and the three left the lab.

"Let's make some more inquiries about Arrow cigarettes," Joe suggested.

They stopped at one place after another, but none of the proprietors had ever heard of them.

"What I want to find out now," Frank said, "is something more about *real* arrows."

He spoke to a policeman, who suggested a museum a short distance away.

The trio spent nearly an hour looking over the collection. Finally Joe remarked:

"Funny thing. Every one of these arrows is longer than the white-feathered arrows."

"And they're not so thick," Frank added. "Whoever shot at Dad and me must make his own."

After leaving the museum, the boys went back to the airport. Winger was standing near his plane.

"All set?" he asked, smiling. After they were in the air, he said, "Well, did you find any more crooked arrows?"

"Not one," Chet replied, "but we're still looking."

That evening after supper the boys joined Ruth Hardy on the porch. She told them that there had been more trouble at the ranch. "Another cowboy disappeared while you were in Santa Fe," she said. "He took his saddle and all his clothes, just as the others did."

With their cousin's permission, the Hardys and Chet went to the bunkhouse after dinner and questioned the cowboys. The ranch hands, as usual, could give no explanation for the latest disappearance. Hank watched the proceedings with slitted eyes, and gave terse answers to all the questions.

"Do you suppose Hank told them not to tell us anything?" Joe whispered to Frank.

"No," Frank replied. "Cowboys don't talk much, anyway. I really think they don't know what happened to the guy."

Joe stepped into the middle of the room and addressed the men.

"You fellows ought to know that the disappearance of your buddies is a serious matter," he said. "The men may be in big trouble."

A buzz of conversation among the men revealed that they had thought the cowboys had left of their own volition to take jobs at some other ranch, and had said nothing to Mrs. Hardy because they did not want to hurt her feelings.

"I'd advise you to stick to Crowhead," Joe went on, "and if you value your lives, stay away from the north woods."

At that admonition Hank arose from his cot and glared at the Hardys.

"Now hold on!" he roared. "I'll not let a couple o' coyotes come in here an' give advice to my men. I'm runnin' the affairs of Crowhead an' I don't need any help from tenderfeet!"

To avoid another fracas, the visitors left. Chet thumped Joe on the back.

"Good sermon, Parson Hardy," he said. "Only Old Stoneface in there didn't like it. Say," he added seriously, "do you think Hank's mixed up in all this?"

"He's either guilty," Frank answered, "or else he's the meanest straight guy I've ever met."

"Right," said the other boys in unison, and Joe added, "I've got an idea. Let's find out how much these fellows know about archery."

"Now you're talking," Frank agreed. "We could make a bow and some arrows tomorrow, and let the men prove their innocence!"

"I get it!" Chet said eagerly. "Maybe that arch-er's right here at Crowhead."

The following morning the boys obtained a piece of seasoned hickory from the ranch work-shop, and spent several hours on their project.

Frank shaped a bow from it, while Joe and Chet fashioned a couple of arrows.

"We don't need sharp arrowheads," Frank said. "Just make the ends blunt."

For the rest of the day, the boys helped with some urgent chores around the ranch. That eve-ning, after the cowboys had completed their work, the visitors mingled with them outside the bunk-house. Frank casually mentioned arrows and of-fered to let the men use the bow the boys had made. A quiet indifference met their suggestion. As one cowboy put it:

"I ain't never had a bow an' arrow in my hands. I'll stake my chips on an old six-shooter any time."

"Well," said Frank, discouraged by the futile attempt to wangle a new clue, "I guess I'll try shooting this thing myself." He strung the bow, inserted an arrow, and drew the string back.

Just as he was about to let the shaft fly in the direction of the shed, Pye rushed up, shouting:

"Don't shoot! Don't shoot!"

CHAPTER XIV

A Familiar Face

PYE's warning not to shoot the arrow was followed by a fearful snorting and bellowing. Frank whirled to see a mad bull, which had jumped the fence of a shipping pen, charging directly at him and the other boys.

Quick as lightning, Pye grabbed the bow and arrow from Frank's hands. With one deft, continuous movement, he strung the shaft, drew the bowstring, and let the arrow fly!

The blunt arrow caught the animal directly between the eyes. He went down in a heap, stunned by the crashing blow.

"Wow!" Joe exclaimed. "Some shot!"

"You s-saved our lives," Chet stammered.

Frank, though grateful, was not so jubilant as the others. The episode raised a serious doubt in his mind about Pye's innocence.

The Indian looked sheepish as he handed the

bow back to Frank. "I didn't realize I could shoot straight any more," he said, grinning.

"You look as if you had plenty of practice recently," Frank commented.

Pye looked at him in surprise. "I haven't had a bow in my hands since I was a boy!" Then suddenly he realized what Frank meant.

"Now look. I didn't shoot that arrow at you in the woods!"

"That's right," Joe spoke up. "Pye was with me every minute on our ride."

"I'm sorry I doubted you, Pye," Frank apologized.

One of the men who was preparing to drag the bull away looked up. "What are you all talking about?" he asked in alarm.

Before the Hardys could stop Pye, the little Indian excitedly told what had happened to Frank in the woods. The cowboys stared in amazement, then turned their eyes on Joe.

"I see what yo' were drivin' at yestiddy," one of them said. "I sure won't show my face in the north woods!"

There was a murmur of agreement.

As the Hardys and Chet said good night and walked off toward the ranch house, Frank remarked, "We didn't learn much, but because those woods have something to do with the missing cowboys, the rest of the men certainly will stay away from that area!"

Next morning the Hardys would have liked to take Pye and Terry and follow the trail of the mysterious archer in the woods, but Hank ordered his men to ride fence. The only concession he would make was to permit the visitors to go with their favorite cowboys.

"We'll meet yo' at the corral," Terry said.

Pye picked out good ponies for the three boys and they mounted quickly. Then the five riders set off at a tireless trot.

They had not gone far before Terry reached to the left side of the saddle, under his rope, and pulled out a small stringed instrument.

"What's that?" Frank asked in surprise.

"My range gee-tar." Terry smiled. "Regular one's kinda big to tote on horseback. I made this here little fella myself."

Terry strummed out a melody which kept time with the rhythmic cadence of the trotting pony.

They rode on all morning, the men's checkup of the cattle bringing them close to the woods where the arrows had nearly hit Frank.

After a brief stop for lunch the riders remounted and set off again.

Suddenly Frank reined in his horse.

"What's that sound?" he asked.

"Yo' got good ears," Terry replied. "It's just a bawlin' dogie lost in the woods. Want to give him a hand?"

Frank turned his mount into the woods, heading toward the cries of the calf.

"I'll be right back," he called.

The boy rode a hundred yards, then halted. The bawling of the dogie had ceased, but as Frank sat listening, he spotted something that made his heart leap. Some distance ahead, mounted on a white-faced sorrel in the shadow of a big tree, sat a hefty cowboy. His big Stetson was pulled low over his face.

Frank quelled his first impulse to ride up to the man. Recalling his father's warning, and sure that the cowboy was not from Crowhead, he turned his horse around quietly, hurried back to his friends, and reported what he had seen.

"Suppose you fellows surround the area," Frank said, "while I question the man. If he has no business on Crowhead property, we'll find out what he's up to."

With the four at their separate stations, Frank rode back into the woods again to the place where he had seen the stranger. He was gone!

The boy made his way to the big tree. The hoof-prints of the intruder's horse were in clear view. And so was something else—a package of Ramiro cigarettes, gaily wrapped in gold, blue, and yellow.

Suddenly Frank was startled by the sound of hoofbeats near the far end of the woods. He sprang to his horse and galloped off in pursuit of the unseen rider.

In a few minutes he reached the edge of the woods. He could hear the horses of two of his companions, who had taken up the chase. Off to his right, he saw Joe and Terry racing across the range as if they were trying to break a record. But presently they stopped, wheeled around, and came back.

"He got away," Joe reported as his horse shook foamy perspiration from its neck.

A distant cloud of dust attested to the fact that the rider, whoever he was, had made his escape on a speedy horse. Further attempts at pursuit would be futile.

Pye came riding up. "Must have wanted to get away bad," he said simply.

"I sure wish I'd got a better look at him," Frank remarked.

"Where's Chet?" Joe asked suddenly.

"Over there," the Indian answered.

He pointed far to the right of the group, where their friend was seated on his pony, holding both hands to his eyes. Presently he trotted over to them. In his right hand he held binoculars.

"I saw him!" Chet exclaimed jubilantly.

"What did he look like?" Joe asked.

"He looked like the same bushy-browed guy that came to the farm in Bayport and asked me all those questions!" Chet declared. "And he was at the El Paso airport with the tall blond. Remember?" Chet looked admiringly at the binoculars and added, "Good thing I asked your cousin if I could borrow these. Thought I might see something interesting!"

"You sure did!" Joe exclaimed.

"It doesn't leave much doubt," Frank said, "that the person who's making the trouble at Crowhead and the one who's in league with the Bayport thieves is the same man!"

"But what's the connection?" Joe queried. "Do the Arrow cigarette peddlers hide out in this area?"

"Maybe their headquarters are in the woods," Chet suggested. "That plane we saw may drop the food."

"And Ramiro cigarettes," Frank said. He showed his brother and Chet the pack he had found.

"We're coming back to investigate this place," Joe determined, "and soon!"

The boys started back toward Crowhead. Suddenly Frank exclaimed, "I didn't get that dogie!"

The party headed into the woods again and Frank located the calf, which had started bawling again. The boy found him mired in a water hole, and pulled him out. Frank laid the animal across the front of his saddle.

Terry and Pye rode back toward the ranch house, with Joe, Frank, and Chet bringing up the rear. The boys, talking over the actions of the man in the woods, found themselves a long distance behind the others.

Suddenly, as if by magic, a black cloud appeared on the horizon. The next moment a torrent of rain was lashing the range.

"We'd better get over this gully onto higher ground," Frank warned.

He led the way into the twisting gulch, on the other side of which was a high knoll. But just when they reached the bed of the gully, a terrifying sound brought them up short. It was a swirling, swishing noise, which grew to thunderous proportions as it roared down upon the riders.

The boys were caught in a flash flood!

CHAPTER XV

The Galloping Archer

THE torrent struck the three riders like a gigantic ocean wave.

Frank, choking and spluttering, clung to his mount. The pony struggled with all the rugged strength of a Western animal. Finally, its forehoofs beat a tattoo on the bank of the now-raging stream, then pulled up to higher ground.

Frank looked around. The dogie had fled in panic. Farther down the gully Joe was scrambling out of the water, leading a bedraggled pony.

"Where's Chet?" Frank called to him in alarm.

Joe pointed around a bend where he could see a figure bobbing in the water. A hand reached out and grabbed a jutting rock. Then Chet hauled himself slowly to the bank.

The stout boy looked forlorn when the others reached him. Pye and Terry had raced back. The storm had ceased as abruptly as it had started, but the water still raged along the arroyo.

"My pony," Chet said, "ran off. Guess he was plenty scared."

"Sorry to hear that," Terry said sympathetically. "Reckon he'll turn up back at the ranch. Lucky none of yo' was hurt, though."

"You can ride back with me, Chet," Joe offered. "My horse is hefty."

Chet looked ruefully at the stream, which had begun to subside. Then he cried out. "Look!"

"What's the matter?" Joe asked.

Chet pointed.

All eyes turned upstream to see a white Stetson floating down, spinning in the current.

Instantly Pye reached to his saddle and grasped his lariat. After a few deft turns of the wrist, he swung the rope out over the water and dropped a loop over the Stetson's crown. Pye quickly pulled the lassoed hat to shore, where Frank picked it up.

Suddenly he started in amazement. "The crooked arrow!" he exclaimed.

"Where?" Joe cried excitedly.

"In the hatband," Frank replied.

The other boys scrutinized the familiar crooked arrow skillfully burned into the leather.

"And look at this!" Joe added. "The initials inside are C. B. M."

"C. B. M." Frank echoed. "You don't suppose the C stands for Charlie—*Arrow* Charlie?"

"I'll bet he was the stranger on horseback we just saw in the woods!" Joe cried.

The same thought suddenly struck Frank and Joe. It was possible C. B. M. had drowned in the deluge! Silently the group rode along the bank for some distance, but found neither the man nor his horse.

"Guess he escaped," Frank said finally. "And tomorrow I'm going to find out where to!"

When the riders reached Crowhead, the boys went to their rooms to wash up.

After enjoying a delicious Mexican-style dinner, Frank asked his cousin if she knew anyone with the initials C. B. M.

"I can't think of anybody offhand," she replied. "But I can call the sheriff."

She went quickly to the telephone. The sheriff told her that he could not think of anyone either, but offered to check with the motor vehicle bureau.

"It's too late to try now," he remarked, "but I'll do it first thing tomorrow."

When Mrs. Hardy related the conversation to the boys they nodded, and Chet yawned audibly.

"Guess I'll hit the hay, if you don't mind." He grinned sheepishly. "I've had enough riding to last me a week!"

"Since there's nothing we can do until tomorrow morning," Frank put in, "I think I'll go to bed early, too."

"Good idea," Joe agreed, and the boys said good night to their hostess.

The sheriff's call the next morning was disappointing.

"I'm sorry, Mrs. Hardy, but I can't help you," he reported. "Nobody in New Mexico—that is, nobody who drives a car—has the initials C. B. M."

When she gave the news to her cousins, Joe said with a sigh:

"Another blind alley. Just when we think we have a hot clue, it fizzles out."

"I still think C. B. M. might be Arrow Charlie," Frank insisted. "And probably he's the person who wounded Dad and tried to shoot me!"

"If we could only nab him," Joe said with determination, "then maybe we could solve this whole thing once and for all."

"I have it!" Frank exclaimed suddenly and snapped his fingers. "Let's set a trap for Arrow Charlie to see if he is an expert archer!"

"Sounds great," Joe replied. "What exactly do you have in mind?"

"Well," Frank began, "I know there's to be a rodeo at the Circle O Ranch. I saw a poster down in the bunkhouse."

"It starts next week," Joe put in. "But what has that to do with Arrow Charlie?"

"We can put up a prize for an archery contest—on horseback!"

"Now I get it," Joe said eagerly. "Arrow Charlie signs up and we move in for the kill."

"It might not be that easy," Frank cautioned, "but we can give it a try. What do you think?" he asked his cousin.

"It's a fine idea," she replied. "I'll even put up the prize money!"

Right after breakfast Frank rode to the Circle O Ranch to confer with the rodeo manager. After he had explained about the prize for the best horseback archer, the manager was agreeable. He promised to distribute circulars and posters advertising the extra event.

The Hardys and Chet were impatient for the day of the rodeo to arrive. Finally it came, bright and cloudless. They reached the Circle O Ranch an hour before the contests were to start in the afternoon. Frank went directly to the manager and checked on the number of contestants entered in the archery event.

"Only three so far," came the reply. "Guess there ain't many cowboy Robin Hoods."

None of them had the initials C. B. M., but Frank was fairly sure, if the man came at all, he would register under another name.

Finally over the loudspeaker came the announcement of the archery contest. A ripple of excitement surged through the crowd.

Chet scrutinized the three who entered the ring. Two were young cowboys, the third a middle-aged Indian man.

"Any of these the one you saw on the white-faced horse?" Frank asked.

"No," he said with disappointment.

After placing the target, which was a straw-filled dummy with a white paper heart sewed to the jacket, the announcer shouted:

"The winner must pierce the heart, while riding at full gallop! Three shots for each contestant. Let 'er go!"

The first cowboy trotted around the circle, guiding his mount with the pressure of his knees. In his hands he held a bow and slung across his back was a quiver.

Gaining speed, he galloped toward the target, taking careful aim. The bowstring zinged, and the arrow flew toward the dummy. It pierced the head as the crowd roared.

The contestant's next shot went wild. The third landed just below the heart.

The next aspirant, the Indian, fared a little better. All his arrows hit the dummy, but none found the heart. The boys watched intently as the third contestant rode up.

The cowboy strung his bow, bringing his horse to an easy gallop. He handled the bow like an expert, drawing the nock back slowly.

Suddenly the crowd shrieked. Just as the arrow

left the bow, the cowboy's horse stumbled, throwing the rider to the ground. The wild arrow embedded itself in a fence post.

The cowboy was too shaken to continue. He limped away dejectedly.

In the excitement that followed, few people noticed a tall, blond man, bow and arrow in hand, stride to the judges' stand. The cowboy signed up for the event. He mounted a peppery chestnut pony and pranced around the circle.

Chet watched him closely. There was something familiar about him. "Where have I seen him before?" Chet thought to himself.

Now the rider, stringing his bow, galloped toward the target.

Just then Chet got a good look at the contestant's face. "Hey, Frank!" he shouted. "It's the man from the airport!"

"What?" Frank was incredulous. He stared at the stranger, who suddenly sprang upright, his feet firmly planted on a silver-trimmed saddle.

With the ease of a circus rider, he stood erect on the galloping pony. While the crowd paid a roaring tribute to his feat, he aimed a white-feathered arrow and let it fly. With a thud it cut through the middle of the paper heart!

"Three white feathers!" Joe gasped.

"Come on," Frank cried. "We've got to catch this guy!"

He pushed his way through the cheering crowd,

Joe and Chet at his heels. Chet tripped over someone's foot and almost fell, but caught himself just in time. "Wait!" he panted, trying not to lose sight of his friends.

Suddenly the boys froze in their tracks. The cowboy had dropped to the saddle, galloped directly to the judges' stand, and scooped up the prize money, which a dumbfounded judge held in an envelope.

Then, spurring his mount faster, he vaulted a low fence and disappeared over the shimmering prairie in a cloud of dust!

CHAPTER XVI

Mystery Smoke

"WELL, I'll be hog-tied!" Joe exclaimed as he watched the swirling dust in the distance. The mysterious archer had ridden off so swiftly that none of the boys could have overtaken him.

"He's gone," Frank said disgustedly.

"Let's go over to the judges' stand and see who he is," Joe suggested.

"Right." Frank led the way to the platform. The registration form revealed that the archer's name was A. Silver.

"Probably phony," Chet commented, after they had stepped down again.

"Yes," Frank said. "Come on. We'll have a look at that arrow before the target's taken away."

They elbowed their way through the raucous rodeo crowd to the spot where the straw-stuffed dummy lay grotesquely on the ground. The arrows protruded like porcupine quills.

Frank bent down and pulled the winning shaft

from the heart of the effigy. After examining it carefully, he turned to Joe.

"It's identical to the other white-feathered arrows."

"Which means," Chet put in, "that Silver must be the man who shot at your father and at you in the woods!"

"Then Arrow Charlie isn't the archer," Joe said.

"Maybe he's the bushy-browed fellow," Frank observed. "We'll soon find out."

"How do you figure to do that?" Chet countered.

"We'll go back to the woods," Frank replied. "But this time we'll make it an overnight expedition so we can investigate more thoroughly. I think the stone with the crooked arrow on it may be a meeting place of some kind."

"Maybe Pye and Terry can come along," Joe said. "That is, if Hank will let them!"

"I'll ask him as soon as we get back," Frank said.

Upon reaching Crowhead, the boys rubbed down their horses, then Frank approached the foreman. He was standing alongside the corral smoking a cigarette. Frank told him that the boys wanted to go camping, and asked if Pye and Terry might go along.

Hank shook his head determinedly. "Yo' can't

take my ranch hands every time yo' have a mind to do some sightseein'!" he barked.

Frank realized it was useless to argue with the obstinate foreman. He quickly turned the subject of conversation to cigarettes and asked Hank what brand he smoked.

"Ramiros," he replied, and stalked off.

"Yo' sure look like a lost dogie," a voice said behind Frank. "What's on yore mind?"

Turning, Frank saw Terry. On a hunch he asked the singing cowboy what he really thought of Hank.

"Mighty ornery," Terry replied. "But loyal to Mis' Hardy, if that's what yo're drivin' at."

"Thanks," Frank said. "See you later."

He went straight to his cousin and brought her up to date on the progress in solving the Crowhead mystery. She backed up Terry's opinion of Hank's honesty. In view of her faith in her foreman, Frank remained silent about the telephone conversation Chet had overheard in the bunkhouse.

"I'll see what I can do about convincing him to let Pye and Terry go with you on your ride. I don't want you to be in those woods alone," she told Frank.

After dinner she summoned Hank. Half an hour later the two emerged from the living room, Hank's expression sullen. As he strode out of the house, Mrs. Hardy came to the boys.

"Pye and Terry will ride with you tomorrow afternoon," she said, smiling. "Hank didn't want to let them go, because he's so shorthanded. But I told him a day's work wouldn't matter, if it would help clear up the mystery haunting Crowhead."

The following day shortly after lunch, Pye and Terry had finished their chores to Hank's satisfaction. Both men were eager to start the trip as they helped Frank, Joe, and Chet with the canned foods and canteens of water. After a careful check of their gear, the five trotted off.

As on the previous trip, the riders became silent once they had settled down to the long jaunt. When they neared the mysterious woods, they went straight to the spot where Frank had seen the strange rider.

"He's been back!" the boy cried, examining the fresh hoofprints. "Or at least *someone* has!"

Marks of a horse were all around the area, indicating the animal had stood and pawed the ground. Had his master gone somewhere on foot? A search proved the rider had not dismounted.

"Let's see where the hoofprints lead," Joe said.

Picking their way carefully along a lightly blazed trail, the five approached an area of sparsely wooded ground, then emerged on the other side of the forest.

"Here's where he got away that time," Chet announced.

"And here's where we lose him again," Frank declared, scrutinizing the hoofprints.

Traces of a horse's hoofs became intermingled with the prints of cows. Soon they were lost in the welter of marks made by the roving cattle.

But the group continued on, hoping to pick up the trail. Suddenly Pye stopped short.

"What's up?" Frank asked anxiously.

"Look! Way over there!" the Indian cried in alarm.

"It's smoke!" Chet exclaimed.

A blue curl spiraled into the cloudless sky some miles in the distance.

"Forest fire!" Terry burst out.

Fear gripped the searchers. If this were a forest fire, it might spread to the open prairie, consuming miles of pasture and timberland.

"I'll ride back and give the alarm," Joe cried. "They can get a fire-fighting plane out here to help us." He prepared to mount.

"Wait!" Terry cried suddenly. Then he added, "What do yo' think o' this, Pye? Forest fire or campsite?"

The Indian stared long and thoughtfully at the curling smoke. He watched for indications of spreading flames but saw none.

"No forest fire," he said.

As all eyes focused on the smoke, it seemed to vanish, confirming Pye's notion that the blaze was under control.

"Would any Crowhead cowboys be camping there?" Frank asked Pye.

"No. There's no cattle out there," the Indian answered. "Must be strangers."

"What are we waiting for!" Joe cried.

The sun was low as they neared the forest, and the sky took on the vivid, darkening colors of sunset. There was no more smoke anywhere.

"We'd better look for a campsite," Frank suggested after another hour of searching.

Joe and Terry scanned the area and found a rocky gulch protected from the wind. After tying their animals, the group built a fire in the bottom of the gulch, so it would not be seen by other campers.

Frank unpacked the provisions, and soon tender slices of tomatoes and ham were sizzling over the open fire.

"Hot diggidy!" Chet exclaimed, sniffing the savory odor. "Put me down for starved!"

After they had eaten, the group arranged their sleeping bags in a circle around the fire and settled down for the night. They took turns standing watch, but the forest was peaceful all during the darkness.

A red sun was peering over the horizon when Frank awoke. Pye and Terry were busy with breakfast. Frank shook Joe, then Chet, who sat up with a start.

After the group had eaten, the horses were fed and watered. Camp was cleared in record time.

"Let's get going," Frank urged, saddling up.

"We'd better go slow and keep our eyes peeled," Pye advised as the party advanced cautiously into the forest.

Presently the Indian halted, and said that they should investigate further on foot. The group walked forward, listening and watching intently.

But the search proved fruitless, and the going tough. Any campers had covered their tracks well.

The group returned to their ponies. Just as they were about to mount, the sound of an airplane sifted down through the dense trees. The boys peered up but could see nothing.

"Give me your glasses, Chet," Joe said.

He looped the strap of the binoculars around his neck and made for a tall tree nearby. Shinning up to the first branch, he quickly climbed to the top limb and scanned the countryside.

Presently a small white plane came into view. It looked like the same one the boys had seen before. Dangling from it was a long rope which reached nearly to the tops of the trees as the plane skimmed along.

At the end of the rope was a small package. As Joe glued his eyes to it, the plane dipped out of sight behind the upland forest. Joe climbed down to report what he had seen.

"Do you suppose the plane was dropping the package?" Frank asked excitedly.

"Either that, or picking it up," Joe replied.

"That proves the smoke *did* come from a campfire," Terry said. "An' it can't be far away."

"Let's go!" Joe cried, eager to be off.

"On foot!" Pye advised. "Our enemy may be plenty smart."

"An' split up," Terry said. "It'd be too bad if we all got caught at once."

Heeding his advice, the five hobbled their mounts and set off separately toward the spot where Joe had seen the plane. They agreed to return to the ponies in two hours.

Frank crept along furtively. After going several hundred yards, he stopped to listen. A noise came from his left. "Probably Chet," he thought. But to play it safe, he hid behind a large log and waited.

Presently a tall, grim-faced blond man stepped from behind a tree.

The winner of the archery contest at the Circle O! Frank's heart thumped wildly.

The man clutched a bow in his left hand; five white-feathered arrows poked from the quiver slung over his back.

In a panic Frank wondered where his friends were. Would they spot the archer before he let his deadly arrows fly?

CHAPTER XVII

Captured!

THE blond man stopped, as if detecting some-one's presence, and carefully scanned the area. When he failed to see anyone, he stalked on through the woods.

Frank wriggled from his hiding place and followed stealthily.

Abruptly the man wheeled around. Frank ducked behind a bush. The archer looked left and right. Then, apparently reassured, he set off again, this time at a ground-covering lope.

Frank matched the wiry man's powerful strides. When they had gone about a mile, a trail seemed to appear out of nowhere.

"I wonder where this leads," the boy thought.

The runner slowed down and emerged into a clearing. Frank, breathing heavily from the long run, concealed himself behind a tree.

Directly ahead lay a small Indian village!

Adobe huts rimmed an open space, where a dozen Indians sat at several workbenches. The man Frank had tracked entered one of the huts.

"Boy!" Frank said to himself. "This is some surprise! No Indian reservation is supposed to be within a hundred miles of Crowhead!"

Creeping around the edge of the camp, the boy tried to see what the Indians were doing.

As Frank moved closer, he noticed that one Indian, seated on the ground beside a low bench in the shade of the trees, appeared to be the boss of the workers. Now and then he left it to walk over to the other worktables, carrying back articles to examine.

Frank watched for a chance to get nearer. When the man walked again to the middle of the clearing, the youth quickly stole to his bench.

On it lay leather belts, watch straps, a silver-cased wrist watch, and several crooked arrow tie clasps!

Frank stared in amazement. Had he found the headquarters of the gang?

This must be the reason Arrow Charlie and Silver had not wanted Mr. Hardy or the boys to come to Crowhead! Did these Indians have a direct connection with the knockout cigarettes?

Frank scurried into hiding seconds before the lone Indian returned. Then he hurried back toward the place where the searchers had agreed to meet.

As he neared the point where he had hidden behind the log, he heard a noise in the underbrush. Had he been followed? Peering from behind a tree, he let out a low gasp.

"Chet!" he called softly. "For crying out loud be quiet!"

Chet looked up, startled at the voice.

"Wh-where did you come from?" he puffed.

"I heard you kicking around," Frank chided. "You'd better watch it. Silver's on the prowl, and there are Indians in these woods!"

"Indians!" Chet exclaimed. "First a bear, and now *Indians!*"

"A bear?" Frank retorted.

"Well, whatever just chased me looked an awful lot like one!" said Chet, mopping his brow.

In a hushed voice Frank told him about the hidden Indian camp. Chet's eyes bulged.

"Let's get out of here!" he cried. "Wh-where's my pony? I'm going!"

Despite Frank's efforts to restrain his friend, Chet broke away in a run.

"Stop!" Frank demanded in a hoarse whisper. "Someone may have trailed me!"

Hardly had he uttered this warning when two Indians appeared. One was the same tall man whom Frank had seen working alone in the clearing. They ran toward Chet. Apparently they had not seen Frank, who now dashed forward to help his pal.

The men gave a cry on seeing Frank, and the taller one leaped toward him.

Frank braced himself for the onslaught. The Indian, his muscles bulging, grabbed him in a vise-like grip.

In a split second Frank broke the hold with judo. His amazed attacker hesitated for a moment, just long enough for the boy to clamp a terrific headlock on him. The Indian struggled as Frank applied more and more pressure.

Chet, meanwhile, had been thrown to the ground. His opponent leaped astride him like a cowboy on a bucking bronc. Taking a thong from his belt, he tied Chet's hands behind him, then went to the aid of his companion.

Frank had pinioned his adversary and was watching every move of the oncoming attacker. When he was nearly upon him, Frank let the first Indian go and threw the newcomer over his shoulder. The man landed with a thud, then bounded up and flung himself at the boy.

In the ensuing struggle Frank fought like a tiger. It took both Indians to overpower him, but finally they managed to tie Frank's hands, then led him to where Chet was lying.

Chet's teeth were chattering. "S-sorry I l-let you down, old boy," he apologized.

"Forget it," Frank replied. Then, turning to the Indians, he said, "What are you guys up to?"

The taller man glared at him. "You'll see," he replied gruffly. "Come on!"

Walking in single file, with one Indian in front and the other behind, the boys were led through the forest to the camp. When they appeared in the clearing, the workers excitedly crowded around.

"Watch this guy," the big Indian said, pointing to Frank. "He's strong!"

As the men gazed at their captives, Frank demanded, "What's the meaning of this?"

A stony look was the only reply.

The men then led the boys a short distance into the woods on the other side of the camp. In a small clearing stood a well-built sapling stockade. Frank and Chet were shoved in. The door was slammed quickly and latched.

As the Indians left, the boys heard one say:

"The boss'll be here soon. He'll fix them!"

Frank and Chet looked at each other, panic-stricken. Just who was the "boss," and what judgment would he pass on them?

"Maybe it's Arrow Charlie," Chet said. "I hope he won't let Silver use us for target practice!"

"We'll soon find out," Frank remarked gloomily.

About an hour later someone approached the stockade door and lifted the latch. A stooped old woman entered, carrying two bowls, one filled with water and the other with beans. She set them on the ground, then untied Chet's bonds. Motioning for him to free Frank's she slipped out. The Indian guard outside secured the door.

With his hands finally free, Frank joined Chet in a simple, but welcome meal. Their unspoken thoughts dwelled on the fate of Joe and their Crowhead companions.

Hardly had the boys finished eating when footsteps sounded again outside the stockade. The tall, grim-faced Indian flung open the door and beckoned to them.

As Frank and Chet stepped out they were surrounded by an escort of six Indians, who marched them silently to a ramshackle hut.

Stooping to enter the low doorway, the boys found themselves in a dim, candlelighted room. When their eyes had become accustomed to the darkness they uttered gasps of astonishment. There, standing before them, was a brawny, bushybrowed man whom the boys recognized at once. He had slugged Slow Mo and escaped on the train, had quizzed Chet on the farm back home, and was the same fellow Chet had seen with Silver at the airport!

Frank's brain raced to piece together the clues of this puzzle. Following a strong hunch, he said defiantly:

"You're C. B. M., aren't you? Otherwise known as Arrow Charlie."

"You're Arrow Charlie!" Frank said defiantly

The big man's evil eyes showed surprise. Recovering quickly, he managed a twisted smile.

"Yes," he said, "I'm Charlie Morgan. You seem to be well acquainted with my alias. Likewise, I'm well aware of your identities."

The boys exchanged troubled glances as Morgan continued, his voice growing louder.

"I know all about you meddling Hardys. Your fat friend here was kind enough to tell me about your proposed trip to Crowhead."

Arrow Charlie laughed raucously. Chet winced, but Frank retaliated.

"Don't think we don't know about *you!*"

"A lot of good that'll do you now," Morgan gloated. "Silver's out looking for your pals now. You're all going to stay here—as my guests—for a long, long time."

"Not when Dad knows we're missing," Frank retorted. "He'll find us!"

"So you think," Morgan shouted. His face flushed in anger at the mention of Fenton Hardy. "I've already discouraged your father from interfering in my business!"

"So you're the one who shot him!" Frank said.

Arrow Charlie smiled evilly. "No, I didn't," he said, "although I'm not a bad shot myself."

"Silver, then?" the boy demanded.

"Silver's the greatest archer in the world. Nothing but the best for Arrow Charlie! Right now I have a couple of friends I'd like you to meet." He spoke briefly to one of the Indians, who then left the shack.

The big man was reveling in the situation. Frank quickly decided to make the most of his bragging.

To lead him on, Frank said, "Your Arrow cigarettes were a clever stunt."

"You like the idea, eh?" Arrow Charlie asked. "Nobody would suspect a cigarette of containing knockout gas."

The shack echoed with Arrow Charlie's guffaws. "But they'll never find out where I make 'em," he boasted. "And if Fenton Hardy thinks he'll keep on looking—well, another poisoned arrow for him!"

"You wouldn't dare!" Frank said hotly.

"Oh, wouldn't I? " Charlie sneered.

At that point a man and a woman entered the shack. Frank and Chet immediately recognized Bearcat—the henchman they had tangled with in Bayport. Charlie introduced the couple as the chief distributors of his product.

Frank scrutinized the woman, noting her Indian features.

"Did you leave a black sedan at Slow Mo's garage in Pleasantville?" Frank questioned.

Bearcat looked at his wife with a start, but said nothing.

"Who took off the plates and filed off the engine number?" the boy persisted.

The man looked at his wife, then blurted out, "I dunno. Not me!"

"Why didn't you come back for your car?" Frank went on.

"I did," Bearcat answered, "but Slow Mo was talking to a state trooper and pointing to the car, so I thought they were on to us. So what with losing the watch and— Well, I didn't want to take any chances."

"But Morgan thought differently, didn't he," Frank asked.

"I would've gotten the car, too, if it hadn't been for you Hardys," Arrow Charlie growled.

"How come you lost the watch?" Chet asked the Indian woman.

She said that while driving one day, it had dropped off. She had put the watch in her purse, and her husband later had picked up the other piece of strap and put it into the glove compartment.

Chet, proud of his friends' cleverness, blurted out the whole story of the watch strap. Arrow Charlie was thunderstruck at first, but when the full impact of how valuable a clue the strap had been began to dawn on him, he became furious.

"Take these kids away!" he roared to the Indians who had brought them. "And if they try to escape, I'll throw you and them together into the hissing crack!"

The Indians nodded stoically and pushed the boys through the door.

Frank and Chet were led back to the stockade. The door swung shut and the bolt was thrown. The Indians padded away in the darkness.

Alone in the solitude of their prison, the boys discussed Arrow Charlie.

"If I ever get out of this," Chet wailed, "I'll never talk to strangers again, that's for sure!"

"Skip it," Frank said. "If you hadn't told Arrow Charlie where we were going, he'd have found out some other way. We've got to get out of here and find the others," he added. "Everyone's in danger—even Dad!"

"How can we get out of this place *now?*" Chet asked dolefully.

Frank hoped that daylight might bring a solution to their predicament. But with the dawn came another unpleasant surprise. As they ate the sparse breakfast left by the old woman, they could hear the snapping and growling of dogs close to the stockade.

Then suddenly the noises grew louder and more fierce, as if the dogs had been released.

"They must be after someone," Frank decided. "But who?"

"What about Joe and the cowboys?" Chet asked anxiously. "Maybe the dogs have been turned loose on them!"

CHAPTER XVIII

A Grim Story

MEANWHILE, after a somber dawn breakfast, Joe and Pye sat at the designated meeting place in the forest discussing their desperate situation.

"What are we going to do about Frank and Chet?" Joe asked worriedly.

The Indian stared thoughtfully at the pine needles which blanketed the ground.

"They seem to have disappeared from the face of the earth," he said. "There's no trail anywhere."

"And now Terry's gone, too!" Joe said, his voice tense.

When Frank and Chet had failed to show up the night before, Joe, Pye, and Terry had set out to look for them. Then Terry had suddenly dropped out of sight.

A frightening thought came to Joe. "I wonder if Terry and the boys disappeared like the other cowboys!"

"They must have been captured by someone," Pye replied. "Terry wouldn't leave just like that."

"We've just got to search again," Joe said, getting to his feet.

He reached into his saddlebag and drew out a pad and pencil. After writing a note to his brother saying they would return, he tucked one end of it under the saddle of Frank's pony. Then he and Pye set out, this time skirting the forest.

After they had ridden some distance, the trees became sparser, giving way to a bald clearing at the foot of a cliff. Before the eyes of the riders, a gruesome scene unfolded.

From the top of the cliff a fleeing lamb came hurtling down toward them. It landed in a broken heap near the frightened ponies. Pye got off to examine the dead animal.

"There are no wild sheep here," he remarked, looking up at Joe. "Men must have chased it. We've got to find them!"

With that he picked up the lamb and flung it over his saddle. "It'll make a good meal later," he said, mounting. "Let's use the trees for cover and go as quietly as possible."

Entering the forest again, Joe and Pye scanned the dense timberland for any sign of Frank, Chet, or Terry.

Suddenly Joe reined in sharply. "Something moved ahead," he said.

"We'd better go on foot now," Pye suggested.

They dismounted, tied their horses, and set off quietly. Presently the sound of a harsh voice could be heard. Peering from behind a thicket, they saw a rider on a white-faced sorrel.

Joe, not more than thirty feet away, recognized him immediately. He was the big man he had chased from Slow Mo's garage! And there, standing in front of the rider, was Pete, one of Crowhead's missing cowboys! The mounted man was giving the tall, redheaded youth a tongue-lashing.

"You left Crowhead of your own free will," he thundered. "But you're not going back. Nobody that works for Charlie Morgan double-crosses him and gets away with it!"

"It's Arrow Charlie!" Joe whispered to Pye.

"I won't tell nothin'," Pete whined. "I only want to get back to cowpunchin'. I warn't made to work in no factory!"

"You know our bargain!" Morgan shouted. "I'll give you one more chance to change your mind."

"Listen, Charlie," Pete said, holding his hands out pleadingly, "what'll happen to me if the sheriff catches up with us!"

"Don't worry about sheriffs, or city cops either," Charlie sneered. "They're a bunch of fools. Fenton Hardy tried to find out about my racket." The burly criminal guffawed loudly. "One of his sons and his fat friend are my prisoners right now!"

Joe shot a startled glance at Pye.

"Yo're doin' an awful thing," Pete retorted.

Morgan looked down at Pete contemptuously. "Well, have you made up your mind?"

"Sure," Pete replied. "I'm goin' back to Crowhead."

"That's an unfortunate decision," Morgan growled. "Just you try to get back there! My dogs will take care of that!"

"Yore dogs!" Pete exclaimed.

"Yeah!" Morgan returned. He jerked his reins, digging his heels into the sorrel's ribs. The animal galloped off into the woods.

When the hoofbeats of Morgan's horse faded, Joe and Pye rushed up to Pete. The cowboy's jaw dropped in disbelief.

"Pye!" he cried out. "How'd you git here?"

"We'll tell you later," Joe put in, leading Pete to their horses. "Quick! Jump up in back of me!"

The cowboy did so and the group galloped off in the direction of Crowhead. As the three neared the north boundary of the ranch they heard howling.

"What's that?" Joe cried out.

"Charlie's dogs!" Pete gasped.

"They're wild!" Pye shouted.

The fearful howls grew louder. Turning in his

saddle, Joe could see the leader of the pack, his fangs bared, bounding toward them.

"We can't outrace those killers!" Pete moaned.

The Indian's face was determined. "I'll fool 'em," he said.

Joe and Pete tensed, wondering what Pye planned to do. In a lightninglike movement the Indian pulled a knife from his belt. He grasped the dead lamb slung behind his saddle, severed one hind leg, and tossed it to the snapping dogs. The pack skidded to an abrupt halt, taking time to tear the meat to pieces. Then they renewed their savage pursuit.

Again and again Pye cut pieces from the carcass to delay the dogs. Their yelping faded as the horses gained. When Pye had but one piece left, he shouted to Joe:

"Wait for me at the fence!"

Swerving his horse, Pye galloped off at a tangent, heading for higher ground. The dogs tore after him.

From the distance, Joe and Pete watched spellbound. Pye urged his pony up a steep, stony butte as the dogs pursued. Then he galloped to the far side of the bluff and tossed the last piece of lamb to the very edge of the cliff. Meanwhile the dogs had scrambled to the top of the butte. Their jaws flecked with froth, the charging beasts bounded toward the meat.

Too late to check their momentum, half of them tumbled into the abyss below, crashing onto jagged rocks. The others seized the piece of lamb. A brutal scrimmage followed, with the largest dog finally shaking the fragment of meat from the rest of the pack and loping off. But his victory was short-lived. The infuriated pack set upon him, then upon one another.

"What a fight!" Joe exclaimed.

"Only three left now," Pete said in relief.

The survivors limped down the slope and stole off into the forest, licking their wounds. Pye rode into sight a few minutes later.

"You saved our lives!" Joe cried.

The Indian grinned. "Mine, too," he said. "Now let's rest a minute."

He, Joe, and Pete sprawled out on the grass.

"Tell us what happened to you, Pete," Joe urged.

Pete breathed deeply and began. One day, while he had been riding the range near the woods, a big man had approached him on a white-faced sorrel and beckoned him into the woods.

"Arrow Charlie, no doubt," Joe interjected.

Pete nodded.

"You're a fool to work at Crowhead," the man had told him. "Hank pushes all you guys too hard. How'd you like to work for me? I'll pay you twice as much as you're getting, and it's easy work."

Pete had been interested in the proposition. The extra money would come in handy. "What kind of work is it?" he had asked.

"You'll see soon enough," was the answer. "And before long you can leave here with your pockets bulging."

Arrow Charlie had had still another argument to clinch the deal.

"Some of your Crowhead buddies are working for me," he had added. "You don't think they'd stay on if they didn't like it, do you?"

"Okay," the youth had agreed. "When do I start?"

"Tomorrow. Bring all your stuff. But don't tell anyone why you're leaving, or where you're going."

The young redhead had ridden to the outskirts of Crowhead with his gear and unsaddled his pony. With a slap on its rump, Pete had sent the animal back toward the ranch house, and started off on foot to a spot designated by Morgan.

"Where was it?" Joe asked.

"Deep in the pine forest," Pete replied, "at a rock with a crooked arrow on it."

That was the place Frank had stumbled upon— a rendezvous for Arrow Charlie and the deserting cowboys of Crowhead Ranch!

"When we saw you running in the woods," Joe said, "you were afraid to tell us where you were going?"

Pete looked sheepish. "I wanted to work for Morgan, an' he'd warned me not to tell anyone 'bout it, 'cause Hank would make trouble."

"So Hank had nothing to do with the disappearance of his men or with Arrow Charlie?"

"No."

A sense of relief swept over Joe. "What happened when you reached the crooked arrow rock?"

Pete said that Charlie had brought two horses and had taken him farther into the woods.

"Finally we came to a big cave. My friends were inside, but they didn't look very happy."

"Why?"

"They were virtually captives of Arrow Charlie, an' they were making phony cigarettes!"

"Arrow cigarettes?" Joe asked excitedly.

"Yo' know about 'em?" Pete asked in surprise.

Joe nodded, then asked the cowboy how much he knew about the Arrows and their distribution.

"Most everythin', I guess. An' I'm sure glad to be out o' that mess."

Pete went on to say that the plastic tubes were brought to the "factory" and filled with sleep-producing gas. The cigarette paper also was brought in, but the tobacco, a cheap, wild variety was grown near the "factory." Part of the cowboys' work was curing it.

"Every mornin' Charlie or his skinny friend Silver," Pete continued his story, "went to the hissing crack an' got some o' the stuff."

"Hissing crack? What stuff?"

"Yo' know, the gas they fill the tubes with."

Suddenly Pye gasped.

"What's the matter?" Joe asked.

"There's an Indian legend about a strange gas coming out of a rock," Pye replied. "I never thought it was true. It's poisonous and is supposed to have killed hundreds of people long ago!"

CHAPTER XIX

Thundering Posse

JOE looked at the Indian in surprise. "Tell us more about it, Pye," he said finally.

At first the cowboy was reluctant to speak about what he knew only as a legend. The crack was located on the side of a sheer rock. From it came a hissing gas that brought instant slumber and eventual death to anyone who inhaled too much of it.

"If that is true, Morgan must wear a mask," Joe mused. "But how did he stumble onto the whole thing?"

"He might have heard the story from an Indian," Pye suggested.

Joe nodded. "No wonder he made this area his headquarters and tried to keep us out of those woods." He turned to Pete. "What else do you know about Charlie's operations, Pete?"

The cowboy ran his fingers through his hair and continued.

"Both Silver an' Arrow Charlie are pilots. They take turns bringin' in food an' supplies an' contactin' their ring of thieves who use the Arrow cigarettes."

"And Bearcat?" Joe asked.

"He acts as distributor, once the gang gets operatin' on a large scale in a certain area," the cowboy explained.

"Charlie flies him around?"

"Sometimes. Him an' his Indian wife. Bearcat's a pilot too."

"Has Bearcat been using a black sedan in the East?" Joe asked, recalling the Indian's watch strap found in the car at Slow Mo's garage.

"I wouldn't know anythin' about that," Pete answered. "But it was from Bearcat's wife that Charlie first learned about the Indians livin' here."

"Indians?" Pye was astonished.

"Not more'n a dozen," the redhead said. "Been holin' up in these woods an' caves for years— livin' like vagrants, near as I kin figure. Charlie reckoned they'd make good cheap labor for his cigarette factory. An' seein' how the place is so isolated, he knew he could operate here safely."

"He didn't count on my dad getting wise to the whole setup," Joe said.

"Or his detective sons," Pete added. "Morgan's

racket was bad enough, but when I found out he was tryin' to harm you boys, I decided to run away an' tell what I know about him."

"You took a big chance," Pye grunted.

All three were weary and their muscles ached from their exhaustive ride, but they could not afford to take more time to rest. Frank and Chet had to be found quickly.

"Let's go," Pye said, squinting into the rising sun.

Just then they heard the sound of a plane starting its engines.

"That'll be Charlie or Silver goin' out on their errands," Pete remarked. "They've got a small airstrip on the other side of the woods."

"A clearing marked with a crooked arrow!" Joe put in. "We spotted it from the air on our way to Crowhead."

Suddenly Joe flung himself upon his pony. "What if they're taking Frank and Chet away?"

But Pye and Pete dissuaded him from racing in the direction of the aircraft.

"We'll have to get the sheriff," the Indian insisted. "Three of us won't stand a chance."

A moment's thought convinced Joe that Pye was right. Pete hopped on behind him, and the three moved over the hot stretch of grassy land toward Crowhead.

Joe's hopes mounted as they drew closer to the ranch. Perhaps Chet and Frank were still prisoners in the woods. If so, they would soon be rescued by the local lawmen. But there was one of their group still unaccounted for. Terry. *Where was he?*

"We'll be at the house soon," Pye said, sensing Joe's anxiety.

They ascended a long grade toward the top of a hill beyond which lay the ranch. Reaching its brow first, Joe gazed at the far-off buildings, then gasped in horror.

Together the three watched in disbelief as black smoke billowed up in the distance.

The ranch house was ablaze!

"Probably Morgan's fiendishness!" Joe thought, his jaws set in rage. "Come on, fellows," he shouted, "before it's too late!"

By the time the galloping ponies reached Crow-head, the place was an inferno. Cowhands were running a hose to the ranch house, but the stream suddenly dribbled and stopped. The fire had disabled the water pump.

Joe rushed up to Cousin Ruth, who stood back from the scorching heat of the blaze. Hiding her face in her hands, she sobbed bitterly at this final, crushing blow.

"Joe!" she cried when she saw the boy.

"I'm so sorry. I—"

"It doesn't matter—you're safe!" She embraced him hysterically. "I thought when you didn't come back last night something terrible had happened!"

The distraught woman apparently did not realize that Frank and Chet were not with him. Joe decided not to tell her about them now and ran to help the men fight the fire.

The loyal cowhands were working frantically. When the pump had failed, they had formed a bucket brigade and were passing pails of water from a well to put out the blaze.

The man standing nearest the fire was Hank. He looked fierce with his eyebrows singed, his face blackened by the smoke, and his shirt torn. But he worked like a demon.

Joe dashed up to Pye and Pete. The three formed a new bucket line, and worked on a wing of the house which was still intact.

Finally the fire burned out. Only the small wing had been saved. Their backs and arms aching, and their bodies scorched by the heat, the cowhands flopped to the ground.

Hank came up to Joe, their eyes meeting for a long moment. "Good work," the foreman said, offering his hand.

Joe shook it. "Hank," he said, "anybody who fights for Cousin Ruth as you did is okay. I'm sorry I ever doubted your loyalty."

"Forget it."

"There are a couple of things I'd like to clear

up, if you don't mind. What about the mysterious telephone call Chet overheard in the bunkhouse?"

"Oh, that." Hank grinned. "My brother down in Albuquerque wanted me to come inspect some cattle, but I didn't want to go until yo' left. Kinda figgered yo' might get into trouble."

"And the first night, when we arrived, did you look into the living-room window?"

"Like I said," Hank replied, "I had to chase some coyotes off. Wanted to make sure Mrs. Hardy was safe in her house."

Joe told Hank about Frank, Terry, and Chet.

"Better phone the police right away," the foreman advised. "Go ahead. I'll tell yore cousin."

The telephone was in the undamaged wing of the ranch house, but the line was dead. Joe soon discovered the reason. The pole on which the wires were strung had burned to the ground.

There was only one alternative. Joe offered to ride to the nearest town for the sheriff.

"Yo' won't go without me!" Hank declared.

But no sooner were he and Joe in the saddle than a thundering of hoofs sounded in the distance. Soon a group of about thirty riders galloped up.

Leading them was Terry, the singing cowboy! Beside him rode the sheriff!

"Terry!" Joe shouted. "Boy, are we glad to see you!"

"Say, what's goin' on here?" the cowboy cried,

seeing the smoldering ruins. Then he added,
"That's what Charlie Morgan must 'a' meant 'bout
gettin' rid of everythin' at Crowhead. Wal, he sure
can't get away with this!"

Suddenly he spied Pete, and stared dumb-
founded. Quickly stories were exchanged. Terry,
while in the woods, had almost run into Arrow
Charlie.

"He was talkin' to some skinny blond guy he
called Silver. They was tryin' to decide what to
do with Frank and Chet. I vamoosed pronto to
look for you, but I got lost in them woods. Then
I headed straight for the sheriff."

"What are we waiting for?" Hank shouted.
"Come on, men!"

Just as the posse and ranch hands were about
to gallop off, an engine sounded in the distance.
Joe's eyes focused on a speck in the sky. It was
coming from the direction of Morgan's Indian
camp!

A sickening fear seized Joe. Could it be Arrow
Charlie's plane? Perhaps it was armed! The posse
would be a perfect target for an aerial strafing!

Joe shouted a warning, and the riders took
cover.

Presently Pye called out, "It's a whirlybird!"

"That engine's pretty rough," Joe observed.
"Sounds like it's about to fall apart."

Soon a small helicopter swooped low over the
smoking house, sounding like a hundred popping

machine guns. The craft dropped sharply and came in for a landing. As the door of the copter swung open, Fenton Hardy and a state policeman stepped out.

"Dad!" Joe shouted, jumping from his horse and running over to his father's side.

Mr. Hardy greeted his son warmly. "I'm glad to see you're safe," he said in relief. "Ruth phoned me you were missing."

The police pilot spoke up. "I thought we'd be missing, too. This copter's had it." He said the rotors were vibrating dangerously. "I can't leave here until I have it repaired, which will take several hours. What are your plans, Mr. Hardy?"

"I don't know yet," the detective replied and took in the assemblage of riders who had appeared from cover. His face became grave.

"Where are Frank and Chet?"

"We don't really know," Joe said, trying to conceal his concern. "Hopefully they're still nearby." He told his father the latest events and why the posse had been organized.

Ruth Hardy, who had come out and greeted the detective warmly, went to get a map. Joe unfolded it. Pete pointed out Morgan's hideout and the arrow-marked clearing.

"Let's go!" Mr. Hardy exclaimed.

A horse was saddled for him, and the party set out, leaving the state policeman and a few of the hands to stay with Ruth Hardy. As they raced across the range, Mr. Hardy brought Joe up to date on his investigations.

The archer who had shot him was the same man who had tried to steal the car from Slow Mo's garage, after Frank and Joe had prevented Arrow Charlie from taking it.

"His name's Silver," Joe said, and told what he knew about the man. "But what about the license plates and the defaced engine number?"

His father said that one of the men working for Bearcat in the cigarette distribution was the culprit. He had stolen a car. Since he knew about the sedan left at Slow Mo's garage, he went there one night, helped himself to the plates to use on the stolen car, and filed off the engine number to forestall its identification.

Many miles passed beneath the flying hoofs of the posse as Pete lead the party toward the Indian camp by a shortcut.

The going was slower in the woods, but after a while the trees thinned out, giving way to the clearing of the compound. The riders dashed among the adobe huts and workbenches.

But not a sound issued from the camp. They searched every hut. Bare! The stockade was empty and the whole place was totally deserted!

CHAPTER XX

Final Roundup

THE Indian village showed unmistakable signs of a sudden evacuation. Ashes of a cooking fire were still warm, and a few implements were strewn about the workbenches.

"Must have been tipped off we were coming," the sheriff declared.

"The chopper!" Joe declared. "They must have figured we'd come looking for Frank and Chet."

"Maybe they've gone to the caves," Pete spoke up. "Since Charlie reckons his dogs got me, he'd feel safe that no one knows about that hideout."

The posse headed up the side of the pine mountain after Pete's pony. The way became tortuous as the woods thinned out near the timberline, and Joe noticed fresh hoofprints in the stony ground. Finally Pete stopped the posse.

"The caves are up there," he said, pointing to a winding path, which disappeared around a bend in the mountain.

"We'd better go on foot the rest of the way," the sheriff suggested.

Once around the bend, the posse glimpsed the formidable redoubts of Arrow Charlie's band. A sheer rock loomed high into the sky. At its base a series of deep caves opened up like the sunken eye sockets of a skull.

"We'll go in an' shoot 'em out!" the sheriff declared gruffly.

"No, wait," urged Mr. Hardy. "A ruse might work and be a lot safer!"

The detective never used a gun if there was an alternative. He had gained his reputation by clever strategy, taking his prisoners alive and unhurt.

"I have some gas here," he went on. Reaching into his pocket he pulled out a couple of gas bombs that were no larger than ballpoint pens.

"They pack a lot of tear gas," he explained, "and I think it's time Charlie and his gang did a little weeping!"

"That might work in some o' the caves," Pete put in. "But one of 'em has two openings."

The cowboy told how Morgan's men had spent many days working on an escape route, if ever an occasion such as this should arise. They had blasted a tunnel from one of the caves right up to the flat top of the big rock. From there, Morgan could command the trail with rifles until his plane, especially equipped for ground pickup, could snatch him up and away from any pursuers.

Upon learning this, Mr. Hardy, the sheriff, Joe, and Pete planned the attack. "We must rescue Frank and Chet first," the detective said. "I'll sneak in alone. The rest of you can cover my advance."

"I'm going with you!" Joe declared.

His father tried to talk him out of it, but Joe was adamant. "Frank's in trouble," he urged, "and two of us are better than one!"

They advanced cautiously. When they reached the tall butte, they flattened themselves out against it. Hearing nothing, they entered the first cave. It was damp and cold. A large stone stood upright in the middle.

Suddenly the sound of muffled scuffling came from behind it. Joe and Mr. Hardy listened, then crept forward. Joe peered around the big stone.

"Frank!" he exclaimed hoarsely. "Chet!"

Mr. Hardy rushed to Joe's side. On the ground in front of them, trussed with strong ropes, were the two captured boys. Handkerchiefs were fastened tightly across their mouths.

Frank and Chet gasped in relief as their bonds were untied. They rose from their cramped positions and told in low tones how at the sound of the helicopter they had been hustled from the stockade and dragged to the caves.

The sound of footsteps came from somewhere

deeper in the cave. The group tensed as a tall, lean blond man ran out, a bow in hand.

Slung over his back was a quiver. Protruding from it were half a dozen white feather-tipped arrows!

Silver stood transfixed for a moment. Then, seeing the detective, he gave a start.

"Fenton Hardy!" he shouted unbelievingly.

"Silver!" exclaimed Joe.

"You're the one who shot me!" the sleuth cried out.

"Yo' can't prove it!"

"We sure can!" said Frank.

Silver hastily backed off, yelling, "I'll fix you meddlers!"

He reached for an arrow, but before he could draw one out, Mr. Hardy lunged forward and grasped Silver's wrist, twisting it with such force that Silver fell flat on his back.

Silver lashed out with his boots, but Frank grasped his left foot and flipped the man face down. Then he knelt on Silver's back while Joe tied the prisoner's hands with the rope that had bound Frank.

"Now get up, you skunk!" Joe said, and dragged Silver to his feet.

Morgan's men had heard the fracas and came running from every direction.

Mr. Hardy hurried to the entrance of the cave

and gave a signal to the posse. They rushed forward, grappling with the men and Indians who swarmed from the caves like ants.

The cowboys who had run away from Crowhead to join Morgan gave up without a struggle, glad to be freed from the threat of Arrow Charlie. But the Indians fought hard. When the dust had cleared, Charlie Morgan was nowhere in sight.

"I know where he is," Pete volunteered, and led the Hardys and the sheriff to the farthest cave. It was the one with the tunnel that led to the top of the big flat rock.

"Come out, Morgan!" the sheriff roared into the cave.

"Come and get me!" a voice replied, echoing hollowly through the rocky chamber.

Mr. Hardy slipped inside. As he did, a rifle cracked, and a bullet ricocheted off the stone wall. The detective ducked, at the same time throwing a tear-gas bomb into the interior.

A coughing noise reverberated in the cave, then fleeing footsteps sounded through the tunnel. Mr. Hardy could not follow immediately because of the strong fumes.

Soon Arrow Charlie appeared, high on the flat top of the butte. When the men saw the rifle in his hands they ducked for cover. He took a couple of potshots, then sneered from behind a rock:

"Thought you had me, eh? Well, you won't get me. I've radioed Bearcat. He'll be here with the plane to pick me up! And this butte will make a dandy emergency field."

As he spoke, there came the sound of an engine. Frank and Joe listened intently. Was it Morgan's private plane, coming to snatch him up?

"The helicopter!" Frank exclaimed.

The craft flew close and began to descend. Morgan raised his rifle, but before he could fire a shot, a machine gun from the copter sent a burst that nicked the rock a few feet from him.

Arrow Charlie knew he was licked. He dropped his rifle and held his hands high as the chopper landed near him and the state policeman hopped out. Mr. Hardy, Frank, and Joe raced through the tunnel to greet him.

"Swell job, Mr. Hardy," said the officer.

The detective smiled. "The credit should go to my sons."

Just then another motor sounded beyond the big rock.

"Morgan's plane," Frank cried.

Instantly the police pilot ran to his craft and moved it under a clump of trees so it could not be seen from above.

Too late, Bearcat spotted the chopper. Before he could maneuver his plane to flee, the state policeman opened up with his machine gun. Firing above and around the thieves' craft, he forced the pilot to give up or be shot.

Bearcat chose the former, and soon he and his

wife were emerging from the white plane, with their hands held high.

When all the prisoners were rounded up, the law officers and Mr. Hardy questioned Arrow Charlie about his operation at the caves. The big man was surly at first. But he finally realized silence was useless. Hoping for a lighter prison sentence, he talked freely.

He showed the Hardys into a secret room deep in one of the caves, where the Arrow cigarettes were made.

"What about the hissing crack?" Frank asked.

Morgan led them to a pit a hundred yards back of the big rock. From one side a white plume of smoke hissed out through a split in the rock's surface. Morgan had learned about it from the Indians and had employed a chemist to help him exploit the mysterious gas.

Then he had hired the Indians to guard the approaches to his cigarette factory. When he needed more labor, he had lured the cowboys away from Crowhead, the nearest ranch.

"How did you hit upon the crooked arrow as a sign of identification for your men?" Mr. Hardy asked.

"That really wasn't an arrow," the man replied. "It was an ancient, writhing snake with crooked fangs and a forked tail. I found it carved on a rock pointing to the hissing crack. Must have been put there long ago by Indians as a warning. At first I thought it was a crooked arrow, and decided it would make a swell insigne for my distributors."

Arrow Charlie shrugged. "Things were going real well, until you Hardys began investigating our setup. I sent Silver to Bayport to put Fenton Hardy out of commission, but it didn't help."

"Who set the ranch afire?" Joe asked.

The guilty look on Morgan's face revealed that the fire, indeed, was the result of arson.

After a short rest, the sheriff and his men escorted the prisoners on the long ride to town, while the Hardys, Chet, Pete, and the errant cowboys rode back to Crowhead. The hands, reticent at first, began talking about Arrow Charlie. When they heard that the ranch house had been burned at his direction, they were enraged.

"I think," Pete said, "the least we can do to repay Mrs. Hardy is to help rebuild the house."

Cheers of approval greeted his suggestion.

For the next two weeks Crowhead resounded to the clang of hammers and saws as the construction work moved along at a rapid pace. Ruth Hardy's appreciation was unbounded.

Then, the day after the job was completed, the Hardys and Chet stepped aboard a big jetliner at the Santa Fe airport to fly home. Mr. Hardy had left earlier to work on another case.

Frank and Joe felt a little letdown as the plane lifted into the clouds. Life was beginning to seem slow already. But, as Chet predicted, this was not to be for long. *The Secret of the Lost Tunnel* was soon to bring new adventure into their lives.

"I wonder what Slow Mo will say when we tell him we started solving the crooked arrow mystery right in his garage," Frank said.

Joe grinned broadly. "He'll probably say, 'I never thought of that!' "